A Book of Kings and Queens

A BOOK OF
KINGS AND QUEENS

Ruth Manning-Sanders

ILLUSTRATED BY
ROBIN JACQUES

METHUEN CHILDREN'S BOOKS

LONDON

Some of Ruth Manning-Sanders' other books

A BOOK OF GIANTS

A BOOK OF DWARFS

A BOOK OF DRAGONS

A BOOK OF WITCHES

A BOOK OF WIZARDS

A BOOK OF MERMAIDS

A BOOK OF GHOSTS AND GOBLINS

A BOOK OF PRINCES AND PRINCESSES

A BOOK OF DEVILS AND DEMONS

A BOOK OF CHARMS AND CHANGELINGS

A BOOK OF OGRES AND TROLLS

A BOOK OF SORCERERS AND SPELLS

A BOOK OF MAGIC ANIMALS

A BOOK OF MONSTERS

A BOOK OF ENCHANTMENTS AND CURSES

A CHOICE OF MAGIC

GIANNI AND THE OGRE

THE THREE WITCH MAIDENS

DAMIAN AND THE DRAGON

SIR GREEN HAT AND THE WIZARD

SCOTTISH FOLK TALES

*First published in Great Britain 1977
by Methuen Children's Books Ltd
11 New Fetter Lane, London EC4P 4EE
Copyright © 1977 Ruth Manning-Sanders
Printed in Great Britain
by Ebenezer Baylis and Son, Ltd
The Trinity Press, Worcester, and London*
ISBN 0 416 57610 9

Contents

1 · Selim and the Snake Queen

Once upon a time – in the early spring time, it was – a young shepherd boy, called Selim, sat on a grassy knoll in a field where his sheep were grazing. The day was bright, Selim was happy, he took his flute from his pocket and played a merry tune. Then out from behind the knoll came a little snake. She was a very handsome little snake, in fact she was a queen and she was wearing a diamond crown that glittered in the sun. And what did she do but begin to dance to the music.

Selim laughed and went on playing. The little snake queen went on dancing. Selim stopped playing. The little snake queen stopped dancing. She looked up at Selim with her bright, bright eyes, and said, 'Play again, Selim, play again!'

So Selim played another tune, a slow wavering tune. And the little snake queen danced a slow wavering dance. So it went on, from gay tune to solemn tune, from happy tune to sad tune, and the little snake queen up on the tip of her tail, weaving her body into quick, merry coils, or slow melancholy coils, with her glowing eyes always fixed on Selim's face. Until at last she cried out 'Enough! Enough!' And Selim stopped playing, and put the flute back in his pocket.

Then the little snake queen said, 'Thank you, Selim!' She crept under a boulder and came out again with a gold coin in her mouth.

'A present for you, Selim,' said the little snake queen, dropping the coin on to Selim's knee.

'Thank you, little snake queen, but –'

'No buts!' said the little snake queen, and went back behind the knoll.

At sunset Selim drove his flock back to the farm where he worked. Early next morning he drove the sheep to the same field. And there on the grassy knoll the little snake queen was waiting for him.

'Play for me, Selim,' said the little snake queen. 'Play for me that I may dance!'

So Selim played on his flute and the little snake queen danced. He played, and the snake queen danced, for a long time; and when they were both tired, the snake queen said, 'Thank you, Selim, thank you, kind boy!' and crept away under the boulder, but very soon came back with another gold coin in her mouth.

'A present for you, Selim,' said the little snake queen, dropping the coin into Selim's hand.

'Oh, but little snake –'

'No buts,' said the little snake queen, and crept back behind the knoll.

So it went on all through the spring time and into the summer time. Every day when Selim drove his flock into the field, there was the little snake queen waiting for him on the grassy knoll. And every day Selim played his flute and the little snake queen danced, and Selim went home at sunset with another gold coin in his pocket. Towards the end of the summer he felt so rich that he gave up working for the farmer, bought a plot of land down by the sea, built a little house there, and kept some sheep of his own. Only a very little house, only a very little flock, but Selim felt grandly happy, and every day he drove his little flock up to graze under the knoll; and every day the little snake queen came out from behind the knoll and danced to the tune of Selim's flute.

'You see, Selim,' she said, 'it's all very fine to be a queen, but

8

one does like occasionally to get away from all the pomp of the court and be a girl again.'

But one day in late autumn the little snake queen said, 'Selim, winter is coming, and I and my people are going to curl up inside the knoll and sleep till spring, when the birds will waken us with their singing. So it's goodbye for a time. Tell me, which do you like best – oranges or apples?'

'I like them both,' said Selim, 'the one as well as the other.'

'Then you shall have both,' said the little snake queen. And she crawled away behind the knoll, and came back carrying a twig in her mouth. 'Plant this twig in your garden, Selim, and it will grow into a tree that will bear both oranges and apples: oranges one day, apples the next. And what's more, with my blessing, it will bear them all the year round. Now goodbye until the spring time!'

Then the little snake queen went down into the knoll, and Selim gathered his flock together and drove it home. That evening he planted the twig in his garden. . . . And next morning – what do you think? The twig had grown into a splendid tree, whose branches were bright with rosy apples.

That day Selim left his flock to graze in his own little meadow, and having picked the apples he went into town to sell them. When he got home he was surprised to see that the tree was putting forth new flower buds; and next morning he was more than surprised, for the branches of the tree were bright with golden oranges.

'Oh, my little snake, my little snake,' said he, 'what a treasure you have given me!'

And indeed it was a treasure! No matter what the weather, through autumn storms or winter snows, the tree continued to blossom and bear fruit, one day red rosy apples, the next day golden oranges.

Now early one winter's morning a big ship came sailing along the coast; and the captain, watching the shore through his spy glass, caught sight of Selim's little house, and of the tree in the garden, bright with golden oranges. It seemed to the captain a very strange sight for a winter's morning; and later that day, when he had brought his ship into the harbour, and was taking a stroll through the town, he met Selim in the market place selling his apples, and said, 'That's a wonderful tree of yours, my lad!'

'Which tree?' says Selim.

'The orange tree,' says the captain.

'Apple tree you mean,' says Selim.

'No, no, the orange tree,' said the captain. 'Never have I seen finer fruit – and in winter time too – it's something of a miracle!'

Selim was feeling mischievous. He said, 'I've only one fruit tree in my garden, and I'm in town now selling the apples I plucked from it last evening: the finest apples in the world – you shall have one to taste.'

'I'm not talking about apples, I'm talking about oranges,' said the captain.

'But I'm talking about my apple tree,' said Selim.

'Orange tree!' says the captain.

'No, apple tree,' says Selim.

'I'll wager my ship and all my merchandise against your house and garden and your sheep and the tree itself, that it's an orange tree,' says the captain.

'Done!' says Selim. 'Call on me tomorrow morning, and we'll see which of us is right.'

'Done!' says the captain. 'I'll be with you in the morning.'

But of course when the captain came next morning to look at the tree, there it was almost bowed down with its burden of ripe rosy apples.

'So now the ship is mine,' said Selim laughing.

'Yes, the ship is yours,' said the captain sadly. 'I must be growing old and losing my sight – or else my spy glass is bewitched.'

'I must get busy picking my apples,' said Selim. 'I'll call to take possession of the ship tomorrow morning.'

'Very well,' said the captain, and went sadly away.

'What a joke!' thought Selim. 'But I'm not going to take the poor fellow's ship from him!' And next morning he went down to the harbour, got aboard the ship, and found the captain sitting in his cabin, looking very glum.

'Well, I've come,' said Selim.

'Ye-es,' said the captain. 'Oh my beautiful ship – it goes to my heart to part with it – it does indeed!' And he blew his nose and dabbed his eyes with a big red hankerchief.

'Cheer up!' says Selim. 'I'm not going to take your ship from you. I'm just going to tell you a story.' And there and then he told the captain all about the little snake queen, and the twig that he planted, and how the twig grew into this magic tree that bore apples one day and oranges the next.

After that, the captain couldn't make enough of Selim. They spent a merry morning together, talking and laughing. And they weren't whispering, either! Anybody could hear all that they said. And somebody did hear, and that was a passenger on the ship, a man called Sir Red, a mean and cunning fellow.

'Oh ho!' thinks Sir Red; and 'Ah ha!' thinks Sir Red, 'that tree is as good as mine!' And next day he disguised himself as a merchant, and went on shore to find Selim selling oranges.

'That's a fine apple tree you've got down at your place,' says Sir Red.

'Orange tree, you mean,' says Selim.

'No, I mean the apple tree,' says Sir Red.

'I've only one fruit tree in my garden,' says Selim, 'and it bears oranges. I picked these yesterday. Would you like to try one?'

'I'm not talking about oranges, I'm talking about apples,' says Sir Red.

'But I'm talking about my orange tree,' says Selim.

'Apple tree,' says Sir Red.

'No, orange tree,' says Selim.

'Well,' says Sir Red, 'I'll wager all I possess against all *you* possess, that it's an apple tree!'

'Done!' says Selim. 'Come down to my place tomorrow morning, and you shall see which of us is right.'

'Yes, I'll come,' said Sir Red.

And he walked off.

Selim was chuckling. 'This is rare fun,' said he to himself. 'If I were a rogue I could make my fortune in bets about my tree! But of course, since I'm not a rogue, I shan't take my winnings.'

And having sold all his oranges he went home, humming a little song of:

> '*Apple tree today, but orange tree tomorrow,*
> *And so my fine gentleman will find to his sorrow!*'

But Sir Red was also humming a little song to himself. And Sir Red's little song was:

'Oranges tomorrow, but apples the day after:
Sorrow comes to Selim, but to me comes laughter!'

Ah ha! Sir Red was a cunning fellow! That evening there came a *rat tat* at Selim's door, and when Selim opened the door, there stood Sir Red.

'Ah, come in, come in!' says Selim. 'Have you come to call off the bet? I should if I were you!'

'Not at all, not at all,' said Sir Red. 'I just called to ask what time I should come tomorrow.'

'Well, say about noon,' said Selim. 'You'll find me busy picking my oranges.'

And he laughed.

'We won't argue about that,' said Sir Red. 'But since our wager must be a friendly one, with no hurt feeling whichever of us wins it, I've brought a bottle of my best wine so that we may drink to our present and future friendship!'

So Selim fetched glasses, and Sir Red uncorked the bottle and poured out the wine.

'Your health, and here's to our wager!' says Sir Red, lifting his glass.

'To our wager and your very good health!' says Selim, touching Sir Red's glass with his own, and then drinking down the wine.

But Sir Red, the cunning fellow, only made a pretence of drinking; for he had put a powerful sleeping draught in the wine. And no sooner had Selim emptied his glass than his head swam, his eyes dazed, and he fell forward on the table in a dead sleep.

'Ah ha! my fine fellow!' chuckled Sir Red. 'That will keep you quiet all through tomorrow!'

And he got up and went away.

All through the night, and all through the next day, Selim slept with his head on the kitchen table. In the shed the sheep were bleating: he did not hear them. In the garden the fruit tree was ashine with golden oranges: he did not see them. The day passed, the sun set, it was evening, it was night, and still Selim slept.

He woke the morning after with an aching head to hear someone knocking at the door.

It was Sir Red.

'About our little wager of yesterday?' said Sir Red.

'Oh yes, our little wager,' said Selim.

And he went with Sir Red into the garden.

No, Selim couldn't believe his eyes, he simply couldn't! There was his tree laden with big rosy apples.

'It – it isn't! It can't be!' he cried.

'But it can be, and it is,' laughed Sir Red. 'And now the tree is mine, and your garden is mine, and your sheep are mine, and your house is mine. And if I could root up the tree and plant it elsewhere, I would leave you all the rest of the rubbish. But I dare not risk uprooting the tree – and so I must ask you to take yourself off.'

Selim walked sadly away. He knew now that he had been tricked; but that didn't mend matters.

And Sir Red was gloating. Since he dared not uproot the tree and move it elsewhere, lest it die, he turned Selim's sheep adrift, pulled down Selim's little house, and built himself a mansion on the site. The tree went on bearing its apples one day and its oranges the next, and Sir Red hired a lad to pick the fruit which he sold all through the winter at a bargain price. He didn't want the money, he was rich enough, but he gloated over the tree, and gloated, too, to think how he had tricked poor Selim.

And what did Selim do? Well, he hired himself out as a shepherd to a neighbouring farmer, and cursed himself for a fool. The only happy moment that came to him during the rest of that unhappy winter was the moment when he found his own little flock of sheep wandering shepherdless, and brought them to add to those he was tending.

So the winter passed. Now it was spring again. And on a May morning Selim drove his sheep up into the field where he had first seen the little snake queen. The day was sunny, buttercups and daisies shone bright in the grass, the sheep grazed quietly, the young lambs skipped this way and that way. Selim thought of the happy morning when he had first seen the little snake. He took his flute from his pocket and began to play – oh, such a sad, sad tune!

'Selim, Selim, if you play so sadly – how can I dance?'

Yes, there was the little snake queen at his side, looking up at him with her jewel-like eyes.

'I am a sad fool, little snake,' said Selim. 'And so I play sad tunes.'

'A fool of yesterday need not be a fool today,' said the little snake. 'Come, cheer up! I have a present for you.'

And she dropped something small and hard and brilliantly glittering into Selim's hand.

'What do you call that, Selim?'

'I should call it a diamond, little snake, but –'

'No buts!' said the little snake. 'A diamond it is, and with it you shall win back your tree.'

'Oh, little snake, little snake, Sir Red is too clever for me!'

'He is not too clever for me,' said the little snake queen. 'If I can make a tree bear fruit one day and a different fruit the next, *I can also make the tree bear the same fruit two days running.* And that I will do for you, Selim. But first I must dance. So cheer up now, cheer up, and play me a merry dancing tune.'

Selim didn't feel much like playing a merry dancing tune, but he did his best, and as he played his heart grew lighter. The little snake queen danced so prettily, the sun shone so cheerily, that by and by Selim was up on his feet and dancing himself: and the sheep and the lambs were dancing, the very flowers in the grass were dancing, the grass blades themselves were dancing, and the sunbeams danced glittering here and there, and joined in the fun.

'Ha! ha!' laughed Selim, as he paused in his playing and flung himself down on the grass, 'Ha! ha!' What do I care for that horrid Sir Red?'

'Now, now,' said the little snake queen, 'you must be serious, and listen to me. Tomorrow you must take the diamond and show it to Sir Red. You will find the tree bearing apples. You will make a new wager with Sir Red. And if you follow my instructions, all will be well.'

Then the little snake queen told Selim exactly what he must do next day. And after that she went back behind the mound, and Selim drove his flock down to the farm.

Next morning he brought his flock to pasture in a grassy place by the sea shore, and with the diamond safe in his pocket went to call on Sir Red.

'And what have you come for, young ragamuffin?' says Sir Red.

'To wager with you again,' says Selim.

'Ha! ha!' laughed Sir Red. 'Can beggars make wagers?'

But Selim showed him the diamond and said, 'I see that the tree is bearing apples today. Well, I'll wager this diamond against the tree and your mansion and all you possess, *that the tree will bear apples again tomorrow.*'

'Done, you fool!' said Sir Red. 'And the diamond is as good as mine!'

'That remains to be seen,' said Selim.

And he walked proudly away.

All that day Sir Red was gloating. He went out to look at his tree many times. It was laden with apples which a hired boy was busily picking. Sir Red was in such a good temper that he told the boy he might take a basketful of apples home for himself. How Selim had come by the diamond, he neither knew nor cared. It was enough that tomorrow it would be his, Sir Red's. He was singing a little ditty to himself over and over again:

> *'Apples today,*
> *Oranges, tomorrow.*
> *The diamond for me,*
> *But for silly Selim, sorrow.'*

He went to bed humming this ditty; and woke in the morning to find Selim knocking at the door.

'A fine morning,' shouted Selim, 'and the apples all aglow in the sunlight.'

'Oranges, you mean,' bawled Sir Red, putting his head out of the window.

'No, apples!' shouted Selim.

'The lad's gone blind now,' muttered Sir Red, flinging on a dressing gown and hurrying out. 'Oh,' says he to Selim, 'you've brought the diamond with you?'

'Here it is,' says Selim.

'Then hand it over,' says Sir Red.

'Not till you've come to look at the tree,' says Selim.

'Bah!' said Sir Red. 'You've lost the wager, and you know it.'

'Come and look at the tree,' said Selim again.

And Sir Red went to look at the tree. But when he saw it, he turned so giddy that he all but fell down. For the tree was so clustered with red rosy apples that he could scarce see the branches.

'It's a trick!' gasped Sir Red.

Selim laughed. 'Call it what you will,' said he. '*I've won the wager*. And now I'll trouble you to take yourself off my premises. I'll give you an hour to pack up, and no more.'

'I'll have the law on you!' screamed Sir Red.

'As you please,' said Selim. 'But pack up.'

So Sir Red packed up and went – there was no help for it. And Selim came to live happily in Sir Red's handsome house. The tree continued to bear fruit, apples one day, oranges the next. But never again did it bear the same kind of fruit on two days running.

The first thing Selim did was to send Sir Red's hired apple-picker back with the farmer's sheep, keeping only his own small flock. And the next thing he did was to drive his small flock up to the knoll to thank the little snake queen. Sitting there in the spring sunshine he played merrily on his flute. The little snake queen danced merrily, the sheep and lambs danced merrily, the flowers in the grass danced merrily, the grass blades danced merrily, and the dancing sunbeams glittered all about them, and joined in the fun.

2 · The Queen's Children

Once upon a time there was a beautiful orphan girl, called Angela, who lived with her wealthy old witch of a stepmother, and the stepmother's daughter, Jutta.

And one day Angela said to Jutta, 'Do you know what I dreamed last night? I dreamed that I married our young king, Fyador. And I dreamed that I bore him three, oh such handsome boys, with hair shining as the sun, eyes blue as summer skies, and each with a golden star on his breast.'

'Pah!' said Jutta, 'What conceit!'

And she went about telling everyone of Angela's conceited dream.

Well, in some way or another way – and who knows in what way? – the young King Fyador heard of Angela's dream. And he sent for Angela and said, 'You dreamed of me. Tell me your dream.'

Angela told him, and King Fyador said, 'And do your dreams come true?'

'Yes, they come true,' said Angela.

'Then I will marry you,' said King Fyador.

And then and there the marriage was held, and Angela became queen.

Now that didn't please the witch stepmother, who thought her own daughter, Jutta, should have married the king. But she pretended to be delighted; and when the time drew near for

Angela to give birth to her first baby, the stepmother went to the palace to act as nurse.

'Beautiful boys indeed!' muttered the stepmother. 'Oh ho, we'll see about that!' And she went about muttering spells all day. But the spells didn't work; and the hour came when Angela, true to her dream, gave birth to three baby boys – such handsome baby boys, with hair shining as the sun, eyes blue as summer skies, and each one with a golden star on his breast.

The stepmother nearly burst with rage and disappointment. However, she summoned all her wicked strength, and cast a spell on the babies, changing them into three wolf cubs. But her spells weren't quite powerful enough, because each wolf cub had a golden star on its breast.

'Be off with you, out of my sight!' screamed the stepmother.

Then the three wolf cubs ran off. And the stepmother put three kittens in the cradle.

So when King Fyador came in from hunting, all eager for news, the stepmother met him shaking her head and sighing.

'Sad news, your majesty,' said she. 'Very, very sad news! Your lady queen has given birth to three kittens.'

The king was bitterly disappointed. But he had to make the best of it; and he was still hoping that Angela would by and by bear him those three beautiful boys. He went on loving Angela until she was again expecting a baby. But this time Angela's baby was just an ordinary looking little boy: no hair shining as the sun – just some dark curls; no eyes blue as summer skies – just big, bright brown eyes; and no golden star, whether on his breast or anywhere else.

Oh then King Fyador turned bitter. He called his counsellors together. 'My wife has lied to me,' he said. 'She promised me one thing, she has given me something quite other. What punishment does she deserve for that?'

Most of the counsellors said she should be put to death. But the wisest and oldest of them said, 'No. Let her be put into a barrel, and the baby with her. Let the barrel be nailed down and cast into the sea. If the queen is guilty of lying to your majesty about her dream, the barrel will sink and she will be drowned. But if the queen is innocent, then heaven will see to it that the barrel is washed ashore.'

So that's what was done. The barrel was brought, Angela and the baby were put into it, the barrel was nailed down, and cast into the sea.

Now that baby boy was no ordinary child. He grew not by years but by minutes. Before the barrel had floated very far, he had grown into a handsome little boy. And the handsome little boy said to Angela, 'Dearest mother, what will you call me?'

'I will call you Vanya, my darling,' said Angela, putting her arms about the handsome little boy, and shedding tears.

'Dearest little mother, there is no cause to weep,' said Vanya. 'You and I are together. We shall do well enough.'

And the barrel floated on: up on to the crest of a wave, and down into the trough of the wave, and up on to the crest of another wave, and down again, and up again, and on and on. And all the time Vanya was growing. Now he was a fine strong lad; and when the barrel was tossed up on to the shore of a desert island, Vanya gave it a blow with his fist and broke it open.

'Dearest little mother,' said he, 'here we land.'

And they both stepped ashore.

Heaven help us, what an island! Blasted forest, moss, mire, and bare rocks; an island never walked on by foot, nor ridden over on horseback.

'Oh me!' said Queen Angela. 'How shall we live here? . . . And what are you seeking, my Vanya, that you go feeling under the moss with your two hands?'

'I do not know,' said Vanya. 'But something I seek. . . . Ah, here it is!' And from under a clump of muddy moss he drew out a shabby leather bag.

'Here is what will save us,' said he.

'But that is neither meat nor drink, nor shelter from wind and rain,' said Queen Angela.

'Perhaps nay, perhaps yea,' said Vanya.

And he untied the strap from the neck of the bag.

Hey presto! Out from the bag leaped an axe and a hammer, each of them crying out, 'What orders, master, what orders?'

'Build us a house here,' said Vanya. 'A royal house, fit for my mother the queen.'

Hey presto! The axe began chopping, the hammer began hammering, and in a twinkling, where before there had been only moss and mire, bare rocks, and blasted trees, there now stood a gorgeous palace, the like of which is not to be imagined nor guessed at, nor with pen written down, nor in stories told about. Inside the palace was everything that a queen could desire or a prince dream of. And in that palace Queen Angela and Prince Vanya lived happily together.

Now there came merchants sailing over the wide ocean in their trading ships; and when they drew near the island and saw the white walls and glittering golden roofs of the palace shining there, they were astonished, for the island was known to them as the Island of Desolation.

'We must take a closer look at this miracle!' they said.

And they anchored their ships in the bay under the palace walls, and landed. They came with their wares to the palace gates, and were brought in and entertained lavishly by Queen Angela and the young Prince Vanya. And having been so entertained, they took to their ships again, and sailed on to visit King Fyador, bringing him, as was their custom, rich gifts of varied silks and foreign fruits.

They found the king in the company of Angela's witch stepmother and her stepsister Jutta. Jutta was giving herself airs, and flaunting like any peacock; for the witch stepmother was using all her wiles to arrange a marriage between Jutta and the king. The king was looking tired and bored; but he cheered up at the sight of the merchants.

'Merchants,' said he, 'you have sailed over many seas, and travelled through many strange lands. Have you anything new to tell me?'

'Yes, yes,' said they. 'On the ocean sea, upon a certain island, where before was only desolation, moss, mire, old blasted trees, and bare rocks – an island never before walked over by foot, nor ridden over on horseback – there now stands a palace so fine that finer is not to be seen in the whole world. And in this palace lives a lovely queen and her handsome son.'

'Ah,' said King Fyador, 'I will order out a gallant ship and sail to the island, that I may see this wonder for myself.'

But Jutta cried out, 'Do you call *that* a wonder? I can tell of something far more wonderful! Beyond the thirtieth land, in the thirtieth realm, is a green garden. In this garden stands a golden pillar. And on the pillar a learned cat walks up, walks down. When the cat walks up, he sings songs; when he walks down he tells fairy tales. *That* is something like a wonder!'

And the witch stepmother said, 'Why tire yourself, my king, on foreign travels, when you should be thinking about the arrangements for your wedding?'

King Fyador sighed. 'Perhaps you are right. Perhaps I will not visit the island. Perhaps it is not worth my while.'

The merchants took leave of the king, and having completed their business in the king's city, they set sail for home. And on their way they again dropped anchor in a bay of the island, and went ashore to call on Angela, the lovely queen, and on Vanya, her handsome son.

'Merchants, what news do you bring?' said Vanya.

And one of the merchants answered, 'The king looks old and tired. He is to take a new wife; and the one he is to marry told us of a wonder.'

'And what was the wonder?' asked Vanya.

Then the merchants told of the green garden and the golden pillar and the learned cat. And when they had sailed away, Vanya fetched his shabby leather bag and untied the strap from the neck of it.

Hey presto! Out leaped the axe and the hammer.

'What orders, master, what orders?'

And Vanya said, 'Let there be tomorrow in front of this palace a green garden. In the garden let there be a golden pillar, and on the pillar let a learned cat walk up and down. When the cat walks up, let him sing songs. And when he walks down, let him tell stories.'

Hey presto! The axe and the hammer vanished. But next morning they were back in the shabby leather bag, and in front of the palace lay a green garden. In the middle of the garden stood a golden pillar; and on the golden pillar a white cat was walking. As he walked up he sang a merry song. When he reached the top of the pillar, he sat for a moment washing his face, then he began to walk down again. Now he was telling a story of *Once upon a time.* . . .

'Dearest little mother,' said Vanya, 'here is something to amuse you!'

And the cat did amuse Queen Angela. She sat in the bright sunshine at the foot of the golden pillar, and watched the white cat go up, go down; and she listened to the songs and the stories.

Now came the merchants once again, sailing over the wide sea and landing on the island with an offering of softly gleaming pearls for Queen Angela, and a bright shining sword in a silver scabbard for Vanya. And when the merchants saw the green garden and the golden pillar and the learned cat, they were amazed. As for Vanya, he went aside and ordered the axe and the hammer to turn him into a wasp. The wasp flew on to the mast of one of the merchants' ships. And when the merchants sailed on to visit King Fyador, wasp Vanya went with them.

King Fyador was looking more tired and bored than ever. He welcomed the merchants with a weary smile. 'Merchant traders,' said he, 'many seas you have crossed, many strange lands you have visited. Have you not seen or heard something new?'

'Yes indeed,' answered the leading merchant. 'We have seen

and we have heard what surely was never seen or heard on earth before.'

And he told King Fyador of the golden pillar and the learned cat.

'Ah, that is a wonder that I would much like to see!' said the king.

But the stepsister Jutta, who sat at the king's side, cried out 'Call *that* a wonder! I can tell of something far more wonderful! Beyond the thirtieth land in the thirtieth realm, there is a fountain which sprays out golden rain from four and fifty pipes. As the golden rain falls on to the ground, it rises up again in the shape of little golden birds; and the little golden birds spread their wings and sing as they fly away.'

And when wasp Vanya heard this, he was angry. And he stung Jutta on the nose, flew out of the window, and went back to the island.

And on the island wasp Vanya changed back into Prince Vanya, and let the axe and hammer out of the bag.

'What orders, master, what orders?'

And Vanya ordered them to bring such a fountain as Jutta had described.

Hey presto! The axe and the hammer vanished. Next morning they were back in the bag. And in the green garden there was the fountain spraying out golden rain from its four and fifty pipes. And as the golden rain fell to the ground it changed into little golden birds; and the little golden birds filled the air with their pretty songs as they flew up and away. So what with the learned cat singing songs and telling stories as he walked up and down the golden pillar, and the little golden birds singing their pretty songs, that garden was the merriest place you could ever imagine.

Well, not to weary you with too much telling, after a time the merchants came again to the island, and saw the golden fountain and the singing birds. And having sailed on to visit King Fyador, they told him of the new wonder. And Jutta, who sat by the king and held him firmly by the hand, which he wasn't much liking, cried out, 'Call that fountain a wonder! I know of something far more wonderful! Beyond the thirtieth land, beside the thirtieth ocean, sits a mermaid on a rock. In the mermaid's hand is a mirror, a round and gleaming mirror. And when you look into that mirror you can see whatever you wish to see, whether on the earth, or under the earth, or above or below the clouds.'

Then Vanya, who had travelled with the merchants in the form of a wasp, stung Jutta on her fat lip, flew back to the island, changed into his true shape, took the axe and the hammer out of the bag, and bade them bring him that round and gleaming mirror.

Hey presto! Axe and hammer vanished. *Hey presto!* There they were again, and the mirror was in Vanya's hand.

'Mother, darling little mother, what in all the world would you most wish to see?'

'Vanya, how can you ask? I would wish to see my lost boys.'

'Then look in the mirror, darling little mother.'

Queen Angela took the mirror in her hands. She looked into it. She gave a cry.

'Mother, darling little mother, what do you see?'

'Oh Vanya, I see a wood of nut trees. And in the wood I see an open glade. And in the glade I see three wolf cubs playing. And – oh me – on the breast of each of the wolf cubs I see a golden star.'

'Darling little mother, if those three wolf cubs are your children and my brothers, I will bring them here to you. Bake me three cakes, having kneaded them with your own dear hands.'

So Queen Angela kneaded and baked three cakes, and put them in a basket, and gave them to Vanya. And meantime Vanya ordered the axe and the hammer to bring a little boat to the island. And in this little boat he sailed to the mainland, and stepped ashore, and found, at some distance from King Fyador's palace, the nut tree wood.

Tiptoeing stealthily through the wood, he came to an open glade, and in the glade three wolf cubs were playing. Now they

were leaping, now they were creeping, now they were rolling
on their backs; and bright to see on each wolf cub's breast shone
a golden star.

Sheltering himself behind a hazel bush, Vanya tossed the three
cakes out of the basket. *Sniff, sniff, sniff!* The wolf cubs smelled
the cakes, they pounced on them, and gobbled them up.

'Brothers,' said the first wolf cub, 'this cake makes me think of
little mother whom we have never seen. And if little mother has
sent us these cakes, we ought to thank her.'

'Thank you, little mother whom we have never seen!' said the
second wolf cub.

'Thank you, and heaven bless you, little mother whom we
have never seen!' said the third wolf cub.

'And may we find you again – if not today, then some other
day!' said the first wolf cub.

Then one little wolf cub yawned, and another little wolf cub
yawned, and the third little wolf cub yawned. They cuddled up
close to one another on the green grass under the nut trees, and
fell asleep.

Vanya came out from behind the bush where he was hiding.
He collected sticks, he lit a fire close to where the wolf cubs lay
sleeping. He took some stout string from his pocket and tied all
three of the wolf cubs tails together. Then he stood and watched
the fire, and when it was blazing merrily, he clapped his hands
and gave a yell. 'Fire! Fire!'

The wolf cubs wake, they leap to their feet, they see the fire,
they try to run, one this way, one that way. But their tails are
tied together: they pull and jerk, pull and jerk, and so jerking
and pulling, they pull their skins right off. . . . And now there
they stand, gazing at each other in amazement, three oh such
handsome boys, with hair shining as the sun, eyes blue as summer
skies, and each with a golden star on his breast.

Swiftly Vanya gathers up the skins and flings them into the
fire. How they burn! So burns away the power of your evil
spell, you wicked stepmother of Queen Angela!

'Come,' says Vanya to his brothers, 'let us go home to little mother.'

And as the four lads go from the nut wood to the waiting boat, Vanya tells his brothers the whole story of their birth and their enchantment.

Joyfully they sailed back to the island. And as soon as they landed, Vanya took the axe and the hammer out of the bag.

'What orders, master, what orders?'

'Let my brothers be clothed in royal garments, that I may present them to their mother, Queen Angela.'

Hey presto! There are the three lads dressed as befits princes; and Vanya brings them into the palace garden, where Queen Angela sits by the golden pillar, listening to the learned cat's songs and stories.

'Little mother, look up, I have brought you your sons!'

But how to tell of the joy of that meeting? No, it cannot be told, except in tears and smiles and happy laughter.

So we leave them, and tell again of the merchants, who, having sailed once more over the wide ocean in their trading ships, and visited the island, come again to call on King Fyador, bringing handsome gifts.

They find King Fyador very melancholy; they find Jutta and the stepmother in a whirl of fuss and excitement; for tomorrow Jutta is to wed the king. The king does not want to wed Jutta; but it is his duty to marry, isn't it? A kingdom must have heirs, as the stepmother tells him daily.

However, the king cheers up a little at the sight of the merchants.

'Welcome, merchant traders,' says he, 'our guests from over seas! Many an ocean you have crossed, many a strange land you have visited. Have you not heard or seen anything new?'

'Yes, yes, your majesty, we have been, we have seen – over the ocean sea we have been to the island that once was desolate, but where now stands a noble palace. And we have seen a happy queen, laughing with her four sons. One son, the gallant prince

Vanya, we had met before. But the three others we had not met. And strangely beautiful lads they are, your majesty, with hair shining as the sun, eyes blue as the summer skies, and each with a golden star upon his breast. . . . But your majesty is troubled?'

For the king had turned deadly pale and risen from his seat.

'Her promise!' he cried. 'My dear wife's promise! I must go to her!'

'Bah!' said Jutta. 'Any lad can stick a gold star on his breast!'

And the stepmother said, 'You cannot go to her: remember, tomorrow is your wedding day!'

'My wedding day was many years ago,' said the king. 'There can be no other wedding day for me. I am sure that my dear wife lives, and that she has kept her promise. I think I have been a hasty fool; I think there has been treachery here!'

And then and there the king ordered out a ship and sailed to the island.

And on that island he found his four sons and his happy queen; and kneeling to beg forgiveness of his queen, he was by her forgiven and blessed.

So by and by they all went aboard the king's ship to sail back to the mainland. And Vanya opened his leather bag and took out the axe and the hammer.

'What orders, master, what orders?'

And Vanya said, 'As we now sail to the mainland, so let this palace and this green garden, with the golden pillar, and the learned cat, and the fountain which sprays out golden rain from four and fifty pipes – golden rain which changes into little golden singing birds – let all these things come with us.'

Hey presto! Up into the air rose palace and garden. And as the ship sailed along over the dancing waves, so along behind the ship sailed through the air the golden palace, the green garden, the golden pillar, learned cat, golden fountain and little golden singing birds. And when the ship came to harbour in the king's city, then palace, garden, pillar, cat, fountain and singing birds swung down and settled in a fair meadow, to the astonishment of all beholders.

As to the witch stepmother and her daughter Jutta, they took to their heels. Where they went nobody knew. Nor did anybody care.

They were never seen again.

3 · Dough

An old woman had a beautiful niece, called Ninetta; and they lived together in a little house.

One day the old woman made some dough, put it in a basin, and said, 'Now, niece, I'm off to market, take care of the dough, heat up the oven, and when I come back I'll bake a cake.'

Off trots the old woman. Left alone, Ninetta stoked up the fire. Then she took a pitcher and went to the well for water. And as she was coming back from the well with the full pitcher – what did she see? She saw a dog running off with the basin of dough.

'Hey, stop – stop!'

But the dog doesn't stop. He runs all the faster. So now here's Ninetta racing after him.

'Stop, stop, you naughty dog! Oh what *will* Auntie say?'

Away races the dog, and after him races Ninetta, along the road, and into the town, and along the streets, till they come to the king's palace. Into the palace races the dog. Into the palace races Ninetta after him, and comes into a grand room, where the young king is sitting on a golden throne. And when the young king sees Ninetta, he jumps down from the throne and takes her in his arms.

'Oh my beautiful one, my beautiful one!' cried the young king. 'How long I have waited for you! Now we must get married!'

Well, you may be sure, Ninetta was quite willing to marry a

king. But then – what about Auntie? So she said, 'Yes, your majesty, but I have an old aunt, I can't leave her lonely.'

The king said, 'She shall live at the palace.'

And he sent a golden coach to fetch her.

Meanwhile, the king's ladies led Ninetta away, dressed her in beautiful garments, and brought her back to the king. The king was delighted. He said, 'You were lovely before, my darling; but now your loveliness dazzles my eyes!'

And he put a diamond ring on her finger.

Now here comes Auntie, pleased as punch, riding in the king's coach. She hops out of the coach, and into the palace, running up to her niece, and catching her by the arm.

'What did you do with the dough?' says she, giving Ninetta's arm a little shake.

The king asks, 'What says my lady aunt?'

'Oh,' says Ninetta, 'she wishes she had a dress like mine.'

'She shall have one,' says the king. And he called his ladies.

The ladies take the aunt away, and dress her in silks and satins. Meanwhile a feast is spread, and the young king leads Ninetta into the banqueting hall. And now here comes Auntie, rustling into the hall in her silks and satins. She skips up to Ninetta, catches her by the arm, and says, 'What did you do with the dough?'

'What says my lady aunt?' asks the young king.

'Oh,' answers Ninetta, 'she says she wishes she had a ring like mine.'

'She shall have one,' says the king. And he ordered a diamond ring to be brought from his treasury. He put the ring on Auntie's finger, but Auntie never glanced at it; she took Ninetta by the arm and mumbled, 'What did you do with the dough?'

The king said, 'What says my lady aunt?'

'Oh,' said Ninetta, 'she wishes to sit beside me at the banquet.'

'So she shall,' said the young king.

Then they all sat down to dine.

And Auntie, who sat on Ninetta's right hand, kept nudging

her and muttering, 'What did you do with the dough? What *did* you do with the dough?'

'*Be quiet!*' hissed Ninetta.

But Auntie wouldn't be quiet. Every other mouthful she was nudging Ninetta and whispering, 'But the dough – the dough – what did you do with it?'

And by and by the young king asked again, 'What says my lady aunt? Is she not comfortable?'

Then Ninetta, losing all patience, answered, 'No, she is not comfortable. She wishes to be thrown out of the window.'

'A strange request,' said the king. 'But so be it.'

And he ordered two strong serving men to take up the old woman and put her through the open window. 'But be careful,' said he. 'Drop her gently, lest she come to harm.'

Then the two strong serving men picked up the aunt and dropped her out of the open window. And she landed in the branches of a tree that was laden with ripe pears.

Now Ninetta was able to enjoy the feast; and the old aunt sat in the tree contentedly munching pears.

Well, after they had eaten their fill, the young king said, 'Sweetheart, let us go and walk in the garden.'

So they went out arm in arm, and as they passed under the pear tree, the old aunt shook some pears down on them, and called out, 'But what *did* you do with the dough?'

'What says my lady aunt?' asked the young king.

'Oh I don't know, I don't know,' cried Ninetta, who was near to tears. 'Don't listen to her, she rambles in her speech!'

But the young king thought it was only polite to listen. He stopped under the tree, looked up, and said, 'I beg your pardon, my lady aunt, I didn't quite catch. . . .'

'*What did she do with the dough?*' shrieked the old woman.

'*Dough?*' said the king.

'Yes DOUGH, I said, and DOUGH I mean,' shrieked the old woman.

'I – I don't quite understand,' said the young king.

34

'It doesn't matter whether you do or don't,' said the old woman. 'It's the girl I'm asking.'

The young king turned to Ninetta. 'Please explain,' he said.

Ninetta didn't want to explain. She didn't know what to say. But fortunately at that very moment along came the dog with the basin of dough.

The dog put the basin on the grass under the pear tree and said, 'Come down, you silly old woman, here's your dough.'

The old woman clambered down from the tree, and picked up

the basin. What did the dog do then. He turned a somersault and changed into a little goblin.

'I only did it to help you to get a handsome husband,' said the goblin to Ninetta. 'Because, though you do sometimes tell a naughty little lie, on the whole you're a good girl, and a pretty girl, and the kind of girl I like.'

Then the young king laughed, and the aunt laughed, and Ninetta wiped away a tear or two, and laughed also.

The young king ordered out his golden coach again, to take the old woman home. 'After all,' he thought, 'my lady aunt had better not live at the palace. She would only worry my beautiful bride. But I will give my lady aunt a little servant girl to look after her.'

So away rode the old aunt in the golden coach, clutching her basin of dough, and with a little servant girl sitting opposite to her.

And the young king and Ninetta went on walking in the garden, arm in arm, and very lovingly.

4 · King Eagle

Now I'll tell you another good story.

There was a young nobleman, called Andron, who took his gun and went into the forest to hunt for game. But he found no game worth shooting, and he was feeling very disappointed, when he saw an eagle with a broken wing perched on the branch of an oak tree.

'Come,' thought Andron, 'I will at least put *that* fellow out of his misery!'

And he was about to raise his gun when the eagle said, 'Andron, don't kill me. I never did you any harm!'

Andron was so astonished to hear the eagle speak, that he lowered his gun and went on his way. But still he found no game, and that vexed him.

'I will go back and shoot the eagle,' he said to himself. 'Then I shall at least have something to carry home.'

And he went back.

The eagle hadn't moved. He still sat with his broken wing drooped over the oak tree branch.

And Andron raised his gun.

But the eagle said, 'Andron, why kill me? Is my flesh good to eat?'

No! Andron couldn't shoot a bird that spoke to him like a human being! He lowered his gun and walked away.

But the forest seemed empty of game: no deer in the forest

glades, no wild fowl among the trees, not even a rabbit crossed his path. 'Confound it!' thought Andron, 'I will *not* go home empty-handed!' And he went back to the oak tree. Now he was determined to shoot the eagle.

But – maybe it was because he was remembering how the eagle had spoken with a human voice, or maybe because the bird with its broken wing was so much at his mercy – whatever the cause, a thing happened that had never happened to Andron before – his shot went wide.

And the eagle said, 'Andron, Andron, what use will a dead eagle be to you? If you have no pity, have you not at least some respect for the King of Birds?'

So then Andron, touched at heart, climbed up the tree, took the wounded eagle gently in his arms, and carried it home.

'Oh, poor thing!' said Andron's wife, Matrena. 'Yes, you did right to bring it home!'

And between them they set the eagle's wing, strapped the broken bone in place, and fed the bird with meat and wine.

My word, what an appetite that eagle had! However much meat they gave him, he was still craving for more. For days and weeks they fed him; and still he was either unable or unwilling to fly, though the wing bone should surely by now be mended. And Andron, though of noble birth, was not rich; in fact he was poor. So at last he said, 'My good bird, you are like to eat us out of house and home. Truly we can't keep you any longer. You must, you really must go back into the forest and live as other birds live, seeking your food from God.'

But the eagle said, 'Keep me and feed me for seven more days. Then I will go.'

So Andron kept and fed the eagle for another seven days.

And on the eighth day, there was the eagle strutting about, preening his feathers and shaking out his wings.

Said the eagle to Andron, 'Get on my back.'

Said Andron to the eagle, 'Why should I?'

Said the eagle, 'Because I tell you to. Am I not the King of Birds?'

So Andron laughed and got on to King Eagle's back. And King Eagle spread his wings and flew up and away. He flew high, he flew far, he flew towards the blue sea. And then he turned his head and said, 'Andron, look and say. What is above us, what is below us, what is behind us, what is before us?'

And Andron answered, 'Above us the sky, below us the earth; behind us land, before us water.'

Then King Eagle gave a mighty roll, and Andron tumbled off his back. Down he went, and down. But King Eagle didn't let him fall right to the ground: he gave another mighty roll, dropped below Andron, caught him again upon his back, and flew on.

He flew, flew. Now he was flying over the blue sea. And again he turned his head and said, 'Andron, look and say, what is above us, what is below us, what is behind us, what is before us?'

And Andron answered, 'Above us the sky, below us the world. Behind us water, before us water.'

Then King Eagle gave another mighty roll, and Andron tumbled off his back: down he went, and down. But King Eagle didn't let him fall right into the sea, he gave another mighty roll, dropped below Andron, caught him once more on his back, and flew on.

On and ever on over the blue sea. And now ahead of them, beyond the sea, rose the green hills and high mountains of a strange land. And King Eagle turned his head and said, 'Andron, look and say, what is above us, what is below us, what is behind us, what is before us?'

And Andron answered, 'Above us the sky, below us the sea, behind us water, before us land.'

Then King Eagle gave another mighty roll; and for the third time Andron tumbled off his back. Whirling down and down went Andron, and into the sea, and under the water. Now he was gasping, now he was choking, now he was nearly drowned.

But King Eagle dived, and caught him in his strong beak, gave him a shake, flew on, and set him down on dry ground.

'Andron,' said King Eagle, 'were you frightened that first time when I shook you off my back?'

'Yes,' said Andron, 'I was very frightened.'

And King Eagle said, 'So was I frightened when I sat on the oak tree branch and you raised your gun to shoot. And were you frightened when that second time, as I flew over the blue sea, I gave a roll and shook you off my back?'

'Yes, King Eagle, I was indeed frightened.'

And King Eagle said, 'So was I frightened when you came back to the oak tree, and for the second time raised your gun to shoot. And were you frightened when, as I flew over the blue sea, I dropped you from my back into the water?'

'Yes, King Eagle, I was more than frightened, for I thought that I should drown.'

And King Eagle said, 'So was I more than frightened, when, as I sat on the oak tree branch, you raised your gun for the third time, and that time fired a shot, for I thought I should be killed. But as from compassion that shot went wide, so from compassion I have lifted you out of the sea. . . . And now that we have settled our accounts for the wrong that was done, so now it remains to settle our accounts for the goodness and mercy. Up on my back once more, and I will fly on. The wind of our going will dry your clothes, and the bright sun will warm you.'

So Andron got up again on to King Eagle's back, and King Eagle flew on. On and on he flew over a wide plain. And in the middle of the plain stood a copper pillar.

King Eagle swooped down and said, 'Off from my back with you, and read what is written on the pillar.'

Andron got down from King Eagle's back and read: *Copper City. One mile.*

'Then away with you and walk that mile,' said King Eagle. 'For in the Copper City lives a queen who is my youngest sister. Go to her and greet her from me. Ask her for the little copper box with the little copper key that she has. If she won't give it to you, take nothing else – neither gold, nor silver, nor precious stones. But hasten back to me.'

So Andron set off and walked across the plain to the copper city. And having arrived there he went to the queen and said, 'Good morning! Your brother, King Eagle, sends you greeting.'

'What! You know my brother?' said the queen.

'Yes, indeed I know him. When I found him with a broken wing, I took him home and nursed and fed him for days, and weeks, and months. Now he bids you give me the little copper box with the little copper key that you have.'

'Ah no!' said the queen. 'The box I cannot give you – it is too precious. But here in my cabinet are diamonds and pearls, rubies and emeralds, and gold and silver coins. Open the cabinet and fill your pockets!'

'These things it is forbidden me to take,' said Andron.

Then he said goodbye to King Eagle's youngest sister, went back to the copper pillar, and told King Eagle how he had fared.

'No matter,' said King Eagle. 'We will fly on.'

So Andron got up on to King Eagle's back again, and they flew on. They flew, flew over the plain, and by and by King Eagle said, 'Look down, what do you see?'

And Andron answered, 'I see a silver pillar, standing in the midst of the plain.'

King Eagle swooped, and alighted by the silver pillar. 'Read what is written on it,' he said.

Andron read: '*Silver City. One mile.*'

'In that city lives a queen who is my middle sister,' said King Eagle. 'Go to her and greet her from me. Ask her to give you the little silver box with the little silver key that she has. If she won't give it to you, take nothing else.'

So Andron walked across the plain to the Silver City, went to the queen who was King Eagle's middle sister, told her his story, and asked for the little silver box.

But the queen, who was King Eagle's middle sister, said,

'That I cannot give you. But all else I possess is yours. Take what you will out of my treasury.'

'I may take nothing else,' said Andron.

And he went back to King Eagle.

'I see you are not bringing the silver box,' said King Eagle. 'No matter. We will fly on.'

Now there was Andron up on King Eagle's back again, and King Eagle flying on, high above the plain that stretched for miles and miles. And then at last King Eagle said, 'Look down. Now what do you see in the middle of the plain?'

'I see in the middle of the plain a golden pillar.'

King Eagle swooped down and alighted by the pillar. 'Read what is written on it,' said he.

Andron read: *Golden City. One mile.*

'That is where the queen who is my eldest sister lives,' said King Eagle. 'Go to her, greet her from me, and ask her to give you the little golden box, with the little golden key that she has. If she won't give it to you, take nothing else, except some food if she offers it, for we are both hungry.'

So Andron set off and came to the golden city, and to the queen who was King Eagle's eldest sister, told her his story, and asked for the little golden box.

And the eldest sister rose up quickly and brought him the little golden box with its little golden key. 'Though the box is dear to me,' she said, 'my brother is dearer. Take the box with my blessing.'

And she also brought bread and meat and a flask of wine, packed in a basket and said, 'Take this food also with my blessing for you must both be hungry.'

And Andron thanked her, and carried the little golden box, with the little golden key, and the basket of food back to King Eagle, who was waiting for him by the golden pillar.

'Good,' said King Eagle, 'There is that in the little box which will make you rich for life. But you must not open it now. Wait until you get home; then set the box down in one of your meadows, and there open it. Now I will carry you to where you can set sail for home. But first we will eat.'

So they sit down side by side and eat, and then Andron gets up on King Eagle's back again; and off flies King Eagle to the sea coast. There, anchored in a sheltered bay, is a little sailing ship.

'Now off my back and into the ship with you,' said King Eagle. 'You have but to steer towards the sun, and the ship will bring you home. But remember, *do not open the golden box until you stand in one of your own meadows*. . . . My greetings to your good wife. She will be glad to see you – you have been away for a long time.'

'Not so very long,' said Andron, 'only for a few hours!'

'So you think,' said King Eagle, 'but time is different in this country. Now goodbye!'

Then Andron got aboard the boat, and King Eagle flew up and away.

Higher and higher he flew, until he vanished into the clouds. And Andron set sail for home.

The golden box is on the seat beside him. What can be in it, he wonders. It is so small, so light – how can there be that in it which will make him rich for life? It would be good to be rich. . . . He takes the box in his hand. It seems to him that something is moving inside it. And it seems to him that tiny little sounds are coming from it: *tip-a-tip-tip-tip, tip-a-tip-tip-tip*. What do those tiny sounds remind him of, he wonders. . . . Ah, he has it now; they remind him of horses galloping a long way off.

He longs to open the box: but no, he mustn't. He must think of something else. He thinks of his pretty young wife, Matrena. What a tale he will have to tell her. It will be good to be home. . . . The sun is hot and he is thirsty. It seems a long time since he had anything to drink. . . . And now he is approaching a small grassy island; and from a hillock on the island a little stream flows brightly down into the sea.

So Andron steers his ship into a bay of the island, drops

anchor, and steps ashore, carrying the precious golden box with him. He makes his way to the stream, cups his hands, drinks, splashes the cool bright water over his face and neck. . . . It is pleasant on the island. He will rest here awhile by the stream, and listen to its merry babbling.

So he stretches out full length on the grass beside the stream, and shuts his eyes against the glare of the sun. It is very peaceful here. *Babble, babble, babble,* go the waters of the stream. . . . But there is another sound too: *tip-a-tip, tip-tip; tip-a-tip-tip-tip.* And the sound is coming from the golden box. . . . What *can* be inside it? Well now, why not just take a peep? Lift the lid just a little way. . . . No harm in that: he won't take the lid right off. . . .

So, very carefully, very gently, Andron, holding the little golden box on his knee, turns the key in the little lock, and puts his thumb under the lid of the box to lift it just a little way. . . . But at the merest touch the lid flies wide open, and out of it come leaping the makers of those tiny sounds: a herd of tiny, tiny chestnut-coloured horses.

Yes, tiny, tiny horses they are as they leap from the box: but as their feet touch the ground those tiny horses grow bigger and bigger, and *bigger*. It is a herd of full grown mares and stallions now that are galloping over the island; and still they come pouring out of the golden box, and still their number increases, until, before the box is empty, the island is thronged across all its length and breadth with tossing heads, and close-pressed shining bodies, and breeze-blown golden manes and tails.

Andron is on his feet, shouting and waving. But what can he do? He runs this way, runs that way, trying to round up that lovely joyous herd. But what use to round them up, even could he manage it? He can never get them back into the little golden box – it is crazy to think of it. Oh, what a fool he has been, oh, what a fool, *what a fool!* Here, as King Eagle promised, is that which would make him rich for life; and he has spilled all his riches on a desert island in the middle of the sea, never, never to be gathered up again!

'In trouble, my friend?'

A voice at his elbow. Andron swings round. Standing beside him is a sprightly-looking gentleman, wearing a long multi-coloured robe that reaches to his feet. The sprightly-looking gentleman has flashing green eyes, and curiously curling smiling lips. 'Yes, I see you are in trouble. What will you give me if I get this herd of horses back into the box for you?'

'Anything I possess – except my soul,' cries Andron. For he sees at once that this curiously smiling gentleman must be the Devil.

'Pah, souls!' says the gentleman. 'Souls are two-a-penny these days. My kingdom is as thickly crowded with them as this island is crowded with mares and stallions. If you will promise to give me what is in your house that you do not know of, I will gather up this herd of horses for you and put them back into the box.'

'But there can be nothing of any worth in my house that I do not know of,' said Andron. 'Except perhaps some little present that my dear wife may have purchased for me in my absence. And though it might grieve her that I should part with it, yet I am sure she will understand.'

'Yes, of course she will understand,' said the Devil with a smile. 'So I will just write out a short contract for you to sign.'

Then the Devil took a quill pen from behind one ear, and a small bottle of red fluid from behind the other ear, and a piece of parchment from his sleeve. And he sat down at his ease and wrote: *I Andron, nobleman, hereby promise to hand over to His Majesty, Lord of Hell and all the Nether Regions, the object that I do not know of in my house. His Majesty, Lord of Hell, will call to collect this object between sunset and cockcrow on this day week, All Hallowe'en.*

'And if you don't come at that time?' said Andron, who was beginning to feel uneasy, and was wishing that the Devil would go back to Hell.

'Oh, then of course the contract will be null and void,' said the Devil. 'But you can set your mind at rest about that. I always keep my appointments. Sign here, if you please.'

And he handed the contract to Andron. And Andron signed his name.

'Good,' said the Devil, tucking the contract into his sleeve. Then he set two fingers to his lips and gave a whistle so piercing loud that all the waves of the sea gave back the echo of it. And at that whistle the herd of horses stood for a moment with heads held high and ears pricked; then they turned and came galloping towards the stream. And as they came they grew smaller, and smaller, and ever smaller, until they were no bigger than pin heads. And the little pin-head-size horses leaped one after the other into the golden box.

'All safe and sound, my friend,' said the Devil, handing the box to Andron. 'You can lock it up now with an easy mind. And if I were you I should step into your ship and make for home. Your good wife will be expecting you.'

Then with a neighing laugh the Devil vanished, and Andron, clutching his precious box, got back into the ship and sailed home.

And at home, before he went into the house, he carried the box into one of his meadows, and there opened it, and watched with delight the pin-head-size herd of horses come leaping out of it; stood for a moment to see those tiny horses become bigger and bigger, until the meadow was thronged with full-grown chestnut mares and stallions and frisky long-legged colts – surely the most beautiful, well-shaped noble herd of horses that you could find anywhere in the world.

Then he hurried to the house to greet his wife, his dear Matrena.

Matrena was at the door, looking out. When she saw him she ran to embrace him. 'Andron, Andron,' she cried, 'where have you been and what have you been doing? Come in quickly. I have a surprise for you! A truly lovely surprise!'

'And I have a surprise for you,' said Andron, laughing, 'I think my surprise is a more wonderful one than yours can be!'

'No no,' cried Matrena. 'It cannot be! Mine is the best, the dearest and the sweetest!' And she brought him in. 'Shut your eyes,' she said leading him into a pretty room. 'Stand here, yes, just here, And *now* open them!'

Andron opened his eyes. He looked – what did he see? He saw, lying in a cradle fast asleep, a lovely new-born baby boy.

And he burst into tears. For here in the cradle lay the precious thing that he had not known about, and that he had contracted to hand over to His Majesty, Lord of Hell.

'Andron, dearest Andron – what is the matter?'

So then Andron told Matrena the whole story, all about his adventures with King Eagle, and his being given the little golden box, which he was not to open until he got home, and how he had opened it, and of the herd of horses that came out of it, and how when he was despairing of ever getting that herd back into the box, Satan, Lord of Hell, had put them back for him, at a price. Oh, what a price!

'And now on Hallowe'en, between sunset and cockcrow, Satan will come and carry our darling first-born baby away to Hell!'

'No, no!' cried Matrena. 'Satan shall *not* have our baby! Surely we can find some place to hide him in for those few hours!'

Now it wanted but seven days to Hallowe'en, and during those seven days Andron and Matrena spent all their time in devising hiding places for the baby. But no place they could think of seemed safe from Satan's blazing eyes. And so came October 30th, the day before Hallowe'en; and still they were thinking of one hiding place and another hiding place, and discarding them all.

'Then I will wrap him in a shawl and hide him in my arms!' cried Matrena. 'And if Satan takes our baby he shall take me too.'

'And I will hold you in *my* arms!' cried Andron. 'If Satan takes one of us, he shall take us all! . . .'

'Well, here's a pretty state of affairs!' said a voice.

And there was King Eagle, looking in at the open window.

'Come now,' said King Eagle; 'gather sticks; rip open a pillow case and give me the feathers. I will build a nest of sticks on the roof between two chimneys; I will line it with feathers. You shall

47

wrap the little one in a shawl and lay him in the nest. And I will sit and spread my wings over him. . . . It may be that Satan will not think of searching there. But if he does I will fight him beak and claw. And perhaps – who knows? – I can fend him off till cockcrow.'

So Andron and Matrena hastened to collect the sticks and the feathers. And Andron fetched a ladder and carried the sticks and the feathers up on to the roof of the house. And there, between two tall chimneys, King Eagle built a nest.

So came Hallowe'en. And just before sundown, Matrena wrapped the sleeping baby in a shawl. 'Goodnight, little darling,' she whispered, giving the baby one more kiss. 'And don't wake until tomorrow's sun is risen.'

Then she handed the baby to Andron, who carried him up the ladder to King Eagle's nest. And King Eagle stepped into the nest, and settled down with folded wings over the sleeping baby. And Andron came down from the roof, and laid the ladder on the ground.

Now all was quiet: the sun set in a red and cloudless sky beyond the sea. Out in the green meadow Andron's herd of mares and stallions and little foals lay down to sleep. In the room where Andron and Matrena sat holding hands the shadows deepened. They looked into each others' faces, and spoke no word.

Hark! *Bang! Crash!* The window panes fell in; and in a blaze of ruddy light, Satan, Lord of Hell, stood in the room.

'I have come to claim what you owe me,' said Satan, Lord of Hell. 'Hand over to me that precious thing you did not know was in your house that day we met upon the island.'

'There is nothing in my house that I did not then know about,' said Andron.

'Ha!' cried Satan. 'You tremble, you turn pale, you are lying! It is ill to trifle with the Lord of Hell. Come, hand over! Hand over!'

'I have nothing to hand over,' answered Andron.

'Nothing?' shouted Satan, and his eyes flashed fire. 'Is your son and heir then nothing to you?'

'There is no son and heir in my house,' answered Andron. But now indeed he was trembling.

'No?' screamed Satan. 'We shall see about that! Come where have you hidden him?'

'I repeat, there is nothing hidden in my house,' said Andron. 'If you don't believe me – search and see.'

'Yes, I *will* search, *and I shall find!*' yelled Satan.

And he darted about the room, upsetting chairs and tables, kicking open the doors of cupboards, hurling their contents on the floor. From room to room he rushed, up into the attics, down into the cellars, lighting up even the darkest corners with his blazing eyes, growing ever more and more furious, and leaving a trail of smashed crockery and broken furniture in his wake, whilst up in the nest on the roof the baby slept sweetly under King Eagle's sheltering wings.

The hours passed: the grandfather clock in the hall struck midnight, struck one o'clock, struck two. Down the stairs Satan came rushing, and out through the front door to search in the sheds and stables.

'Courage!' whispered Andron to Matrena. 'The night is passing.'

'But it is still night,' whispered Matrena. 'And dawn is yet a long way off! And oh, if baby should wake and cry?'

'Then King Eagle will fight with beak and claw,' whispered Andron.

But he thought, 'Can even King Eagle defeat the Devil?' And he reproached himself bitterly. 'Oh, my good and kind King Eagle,' he thought, 'Have I brought you to this pass – that for my folly the Devil should take your life?'

Crash! Crash! Crash! Out among the empty sheds and stables the Devil was stampeding, breaking in the doors, overturning the disused mangers, heaving up paving stones. Now he was rushing round the garden, poking under the bushes and among

D

the rose beds. And as he went from bush to bush, from flower bed to flower bed, bushes and flowers flashed out for a moment clear as daylight, lit by the blaze of his eyes, and then faded again into the darkness of night.

Then Andron plucked up courage and went to stand at the open door. 'You may as well give up,' he shouted, 'there is nothing hidden in my garden.'

Satan gave a scream and rushed round to the back of the house. He saw the ladder lying at the bottom of the wall. 'Ho! Ho!' he shrieked. 'So it's up on the roof you've hidden him, is it?'

And he set the ladder against the wall and began to climb.

'Oh, if dawn would but come!' thought Matrena. 'If dawn would but come!' And then she had another thought: the contract had said nothing about dawn; it said *between sunset and cockcrow.* So now, if only the cocks would crow, Satan must go away empty-handed! 'They *shall* crow!' thought Matrena. And she lit a lantern and ran out into the fowl house, where perched on rails under the low roof the cocks and hens slept peacefully, heads tucked under wings.

Matrena slapped the grey cock, the masterful one, on his humped back. She flashed the lantern to and fro in front of him. 'Wake up and crow, you sluggard!' she cried. 'The dawn is coming!'

But the grey cock did not think the dawn was coming. He shuffled a little with his feet and slept on.

Matrena slapped the black cock, the thick-feathered one. 'Wake up, wake up!' she cried. 'Dawn is coming!'

But the black cock knew that dawn was not coming. He shuffled a little with his feet and slept on.

Matrena slapped the white cock, the handsome one. 'Wake up, wake up and crow, you sluggard, dawn is in the sky!'

But the white cock knew that dawn was not in the sky. He shuffled a little with his feet and slept on.

So then Matrena opened wide her mouth and screamed with all her might, '*Cock-a-doodle-doo-oo-oo!*'

The grey cock, the masterful one, stirred on his perch. He blinked, he stood up, he stretched out his neck, he opened wide his beak, *Cock-a-doodle-doo-oo!*

The black cock, the thick-feathered one, woke. He blinked, he stood up, he stretched out his neck, he opened wide his beak, *Cock-a-doodle-doo-oo!*

The white cock, the handsome one, woke. He blinked, he stood up, he stretched out his neck, he opened wide his beak, *Cock-a-doodle-doo-oo-oo!*

'*Cock-a-doodle-doo!*' cried Matrena triumphantly. And '*Cock-a-doodle-doo,*' cried all three cocks, '*Cock-a-doodle-doo! Cock-a-doodle-doo-oo-oo!*'

Meanwhile, at the top of the ladder against the roof stood Satan, Lord of Hell, His fiery eyes lit up King Eagle, crouched upon the nest. 'Ho, ho, what have we here? With your permission I should like to enquire,' said Satan, stretching out his long-nailed hand.

But King Eagle seized upon the long-nailed hand, and pecked it savagely. 'Now comes the fight!' thought King Eagle. . . .

But hark – what was that? Down in the fowl house a riot of crowing. *Cock-a-doodle-doo! Cock-a-doodle-doo! Cock-a-doodle-doo-oo-oo!*

'Cock crow, and the game is up! Time to go home, my friend,' said King Eagle.

'*Ah, ah, ah!*' Satan kicked the ladder with his hoofed foot. The ladder fell with a crash. Satan leaped into the air and fled away to Hell. Matrena came out of the fowl house, laughing and crying. Andron set the ladder against the wall once more, climbed up and lifted the baby out of the nest.

'Trust a woman's wit!' laughed King Eagle. 'And now good-bye. I'll look in from time to time to see how you are doing. Now, now, no need for thanks. Live wisely, live happily, and may all go well with you now and forever!'

And all did go well for Andron and Matrena and their little son. The herd of chestnut mares and stallions and little foals increased and multiplied. And from being a penniless nobleman, Andron became a rich one, renowned through all the realm for his breed of beautiful horses. To possess one or more of these horses was the ambition of kings and emperors, who thought no sum too great to pay for them. So that Andron was able to add gold to gold, and never ceased to bless the day when he took pity on the broken-winged King Eagle, and brought him home to feed and nurse him back to health.

5 · The Monster with Seven Heads

It is said that there were two kings, a King of the West, and a King of the East, and these two kings were brothers. It is said that the King of the East was called Amdriam Bahooka, and that he was rich, and proud and boastful of his riches. But it is also said that close to King Amdriam Bahooka's house there was a deep pool, and in the pool lived the Monster with Seven Heads. And so, it is said, no one would go near the king's house, for fear of the Monster.

So it is said that King Amdriam Bahooka decided to summon the people to a feast, that they might look upon his riches. And he spread out his treasures in front of his house for all to admire. He spread out his gold and his silver and his jewels. He spread out his embroidered sitting mats, and his velvet cushions, and his coloured blankets, and his polished weapons, and his costly dishes and cooking pots, and his wine jars and his drinking cups and food of many kinds. And it is said that when all was ready he called his slave, Koto Fananasia, to him and spoke thus, 'Go, Koto Fananasia, summon my people to the feast.'

So Koto Fananasia took a drum and went into the country, beating his drum and calling:

'Oh, people of King Amdriam Bahooka, eh!
Oh, people of King Amdriam Bahooka, eh!
I call, I call,

It is you whom I call,
I come to call you!
I call you to the feast of my master, King Amdriam Bahooka.
The treasure of King Amdriam Bahooka, one says, is celebrated.
There is no one to see it.
The food of King Amdriam Bahooka, one says, is celebrated.
There is no one to eat it.
The wine of King Amdriam Bahooka, one says, is unequalled.
There is no one to drink it.
Oh, people of King Amdriam Bahooka, eh!
Oh, people of King Amdriam Bahooka, eh!
I call, I call,
It is you whom I call,
I call you to the feast of my master, King Amdriam Bahooka.'

But it is said that the people made answer thus, 'Oh, good Koto Fananasia, say to the king that we dare not come, because of the Monster with Seven Heads. We dare not pass the pool, lest the Monster rise up out of the water and devour us.'

So Koto Fananasia returned to the king and said, 'The people will not come because of the Monster.'

Then King Amdriam Bahooka beat his breast in wrath, and cried out, 'Is it thus that my people flout me? *Me*, the great king! If the people will not come, go, summon the animals to my feast.'

So Koto Fananasia went again into the country, beating his drum, and calling the animals to the king's feast. He called both the big and the small, both the wild and the tame, the beasts of the forests, the beasts of the fields, and the little animals that burrow in the earth. But they all answered him in the like manner, 'We dare not come, we dare not pass the pool, lest the Monster with Seven Heads rise up out of the water and devour us.'

So Koto Fananasia returned to the king and said, 'The animals will not come, because of the Monster.'

And again King Amdriam Bahooka beat his breast in wrath, and cried, 'If the animals will not come, go, call the trees and the grasses and the rocks to my feast.'

So Koto Fananasia went to call these things.

But the trees said, 'We cannot come, our roots are too deep in the ground. And the grasses said, 'We cannot come, lest on the way the sun burn up our roots and we wither.'

And the rocks said, 'We do not move from our beds at any king's command.'

And when Koto Fananasia returned to the king and gave him these answers, the king raved, 'Am I not king? Shall all things disobey me? Let us then see if the Monster with Seven Heads is not more obedient than my people! Go, call the Seven-Headed Monster to my feast!'

So Koto Fananasia went in fear and trembling to the pool, and beat his drum and called:

'Oh, Monster with Seven Heads, eh!
Oh, Monster with Seven Heads, eh!
I call, I call, it is you whom I call,
I call you to the feast of my master, King Amdriam Bahooka!'

Then the waters of the pool churned up in muddy circles, and the Monster with Seven Heads rose out of the pool, opened wide the mouth of his first head, and swallowed down Koto Fananasia with his drum. And the Monster's six other heads called in a roar of voices, 'We also want food! Give us to eat! Give us to eat!'

So the Monster made haste, and came to the house of King Amdriam Bahooka. The King was standing at his door; and the treasure, and the sitting mats, and the wines, and the rich foods were spread out in the court. And the Monster with Seven Heads opened wide the mouth of his second head, and swallowed down King Amdriam Bahooka.

Then the Monster's five other heads called out in a roar of voices, 'We also want food! Give us to eat! Give us to eat!'

And the Monster's first and second heads answered, 'Eat your fill – here is plenty.'

So the Monster's third head opened wide its mouth, and swallowed down the embroidered sitting mats, and the velvet cushions, and the coloured blankets.

And the Monster's fourth head opened wide its mouth, and swallowed down the gold and the silver and the jewels and the polished weapons.

And the Monster's fifth head opened wide its mouth, and swallowed down the costly dishes and the rich foods.

And the Monster's sixth head opened wide its mouth, and swallowed down the wine jars and the drinking cups.

And the Monster's seventh head rolled its eyes this way and that way, and roared out, 'I also would eat – but there is nothing left!'

And the other six heads answered, 'Stretch your mouth! Stretch it! Stretch it! The house of King Amdriam Bahooka is left, with all that is in it.'

So the seventh head stretched its mouth, and caught King Amdriam Bahooka's house in its strong jaws, and swallowed it. And a great sigh went up from all the seven heads. 'Now hunger is satisfied. Now comes sleep.'

So the Seven-Headed Monster went back to the pool, and sank down into its muddy depths, and slept.

Now it is said that King Amdriam Bahooka had a beautiful young daughter, called Minamina. And at the coming of the Monster, the Princess Minamina had run to hide herself in the bushes, taking her slave girl with her. And the Monster had not seen them. So now, when the Monster went back into the pool, the princess came out of the bushes, and spoke thus, 'Here is no dwelling place! Come, we will go to my uncle, the King of the West.'

So the two girls set off. And when they had walked a long way, they sat down to rest. And the slave girl, who was big and strong, put her hands about the throat of the little princess, and said, 'Give me your rich jewelled robe, and take my cotton one.'

So, fearing for her life, the little princess changed robes with the slave girl. And the slave girl said, 'Now I am the princess and you are the slave. If you tell your uncle otherwise, I will kill you.'

And it is said that after resting a little while, the girls got up and went on their way, and came to the dwelling of Princess Minamina's uncle, the King of the West.

Then the slave girl spoke sharply to Princess Minamina and said, 'Keep behind me, scum!' And she went in and found the King of the West at dinner.

And seeing the slave girl in her rich jewelled robe, the King of the West stood up and said, 'Surely this is my niece, Minamina! Come, my niece, sit down and tell me all your news.'

Then the slave girl told the King of the West all that had happened. And the King of the West mourned over the fate of his brother; and thinking the slave girl to be the princess, he said to her, 'Now you shall live here, and be to me as a daughter.'

But, as the days passed, the King of the West was troubled in his mind, thinking, 'Surely my niece has been badly reared! She has not the manners of a princess! She is clumsy and rude, and she beats her little slave girl without cause. I do not like to see it.'

Now the King of the West had many rice fields. And the little birds, the little fody of the forest, were eating the rice. So the King of the West said to the one he took to be the slave girl, but who was really the Princess Minamina, 'Go out into the rice fields, my girl, and scare away the fody.'

Then Princess Minamina went into the fields. And when the little birds, the fody, came flying out of the forest, she spoke to them thus:

'Eh, you little fody of the forest, eh!
Eh, you little fody of the forest, eh!
Do not eat the rice of my uncle, the King of the West.
It is I who ask it of you, little fody, eh,
I, the Princess Minamina.

But Princess Minamina has become a slave,
And the one who was a slave is now a rich princess.
Tell me, little fody of the forest, eh,
Tell me, should such things be?'

And when the fody of the forest heard these words, they chirruped out, 'No, no, no! Such things are very wrong!'

Then they spread their little wings, and flew back into the forest.

Princess Minamina went to the fields for many days. And always when the little fody of the forest came to eat the rice, she spoke the same words to them. And always they made the same answer, and spread their little wings and flew away.

Now it is said that one day the King of the West went himself to the rice fields to see how his crop was doing. And the Princess Minamina, who was talking to the fody, did not see him, for she had her back to him, and he was treading lightly. But he saw her, and he heard the words she spoke. And he said to himself, 'There is something wrong here!' So he stepped up to the princess, touched her arm, and said, 'Little one – who are you?'

But the princess was frightened, and answered, 'Oh, my lord king – do you not see? I am a poor slave.'

And the King of the West said, 'Then why do the birds, the little fody of the forest, think differently?'

And the princess answered, 'Oh, my lord king, do not ask me – I cannot tell you.'

The King of the West went away very troubled. And he said to himself, 'Which girl then is really my niece? The large rough one, or the little gentle one? I must put them to the test. I will tell them to call my Black Bull, my wise one. If the large rough one calls, and he comes to her, then it is she who is my niece. But if he will not come to her, but comes to the little gentle one, then this little gentle one is my niece.'

So it is said that next day he took the two girls to the place where the Black Bull was grazing, and put them to stand under a palm tree. Then he said to the large rough one, the false princess, the slave girl, 'Call my Black Bull to come to you, for he is friendly.'

And the slave girl began to call in her loud, rough voice:

> *'Oh, the Black, eh!*
> *Oh, the Black, eh!*
> *Come here quickly! Come here!*
> *It is I, your mistress, calling you!'*

But the Black Bull did not lift his head. He went on grazing.

And the King of the West said, 'This is most strange! Why does he not come?'

'It must be that he does not hear me,' said the slave girl. And she began to shout in her great rough voice:

> *'Oh, you Black Bull, eh!*
> *Oh, you Black Bull, eh!*
> *Come, come, come, come —*
> *Do you not hear your mistress calling?'*

But the great Black Bull shook his ears, and turned his back, and walked farther off.

Then the King of the West said to the Princess Minamina, 'You call, my gentle little slave girl.'

And Princess Minamina held out her hand, and called in her little tender voice:

> *'Oh, the Black, eh!*
> *Oh, the Black, eh!*
> *Come! Come!*
> *Though I am now but a slave, yet come!*
> *Come to me, dear Black!'*

And the great Black Bull turned and came running to her, and rubbed his head against her hand.

Then the King of the West grasped the false princess, the slave girl, by the shoulder and shook her, saying, 'Who are you? I do

not think you can be my niece! I do not think you can be a
princess! Come, tell me the truth, or I will slay you!'

And the slave girl began to howl in terror, and told who she
really was. And the King of the West said, 'Go from my sight!'
So she fled away – no one knows where. But the Princess
Minamina went back with the King of the West to his house.
And the King of the West said, 'Now little pretty one, you shall
be to me as a daughter, and live happily.'

But the Princess Minamina answered, 'Oh, my uncle, how can
I live happily? By night I dream of the Monster with Seven
Heads; by day I think of my father. I cannot rest until I know
whether he is still alive, or whether the Monster has devoured
him.'

And the King of the West said, 'Then we will journey to the
East and find out. For I, too, am troubled over the fate of my
brother.'

So they set out, each riding on a sure-footed stallion. They
travelled swiftly. But you who read, and I who tell, will travel
more swiftly still. We will travel back in time, and arrive in the
Kingdom of the East at the moment when the Monster with
Seven Heads, having swallowed down the slave Koto Fananasia,
and King Amdriam Bahooka, and the king's house, and all the
king's possessions, now with his stomach full to bursting, goes
back into his pool, and sinks down under the water to sleep.

Now it is said that when King Amdriam Bahooka found himself inside the Monster's great stomach, with all his goods and
chattels scattered round him, he sat down in a corner and wept.

But Koto Fananasia still had his drum, and when *he* found
himself in the darkness of the Monster's huge stomach, it is said
that he began to beat his drum, and stamp with his feet, and to
call out very loudly:

'*Oh, thunder and lightning, eh!*
Oh, thunder and lightning, eh!
Oh, winds of heaven, eh!

Oh, north wind and south wind and east wind and west wind, eh!
I call, I call,
It is you whom I call!
Let not the Monster rest!
Roar, you thunder,
Flash, you lightning,
And you, oh, winds,
Take up the water of the pool in your fists,
Beat it, toss it, whirl it this way, whirl it that way,
Let not the Monster rest!
Oh, thunder and lightning, eh!
Oh, winds of heaven, eh!
I call, I call,
Out of the Monster's stomach I call,
Let not the Monster rest!'

And the Monster blinked with his fourteen eyes, and growled out of his seven throats, 'Be quiet in there, you slave, Koto Fananasia! I wish to sleep!'

But it is said that Koto Fananasia would not be quiet: he stamped the harder, and beat his drum more vigorously, and shouted the louder. And there arose a mighty storm. Lightning flashed from end to end of the sky, thunder boomed and rattled, the four winds shrieked and howled; they stirred the pool to its muddy depths, they churned up the water in great waves; the waves beat against the Monster's fourteen blinking eyes, and swirled into the Monster's seven gaping mouths; and the Monster's seven voices roared out, 'Here is no resting place, we must get us from the pool, and find a shelter where we may sleep.'

So the Monster rose up out of the pool, and scrambled on to the bank, with all his fourteen eyes blinking at the lightning, and all his fourteen ears deafened by the thunder claps. And it is said that even as his blinking eyes looked round to find some sheltered place where he might sleep, the lightning fell upon him, and struck him dead.

Then, with one last hollow mutter of thunder, it is said, the storm drifted away. . . .

In the dead Monster's stomach King Amdriam Bahooka sat huddled, shedding tears of terror. But Koto Fananasia took the king in his arms, and lifted him out of the Monster's stomach, and carried him up through one of the Monster's throats, and out through one of the Monster's gaping mouths, set him down under a bamboo tree, and spoke thus:

Oh, King Amdriam Bahooka, eh!
Oh, King Amdriam Bahooka, eh!
Open your eyes and look about you,
The Monster with Seven Heads, one says, is dead,
It was the lightning, one says, that struck him down,
And it is I, your slave, Koto Fananasia, who brings you the glad news,
It is I, your slave, who speaks.'

So then it is said that the King cheered up. And Koto Fananasia left him sitting under the bamboo tree, and went through the country, beating his drum, and calling to the people, telling them that the Monster with Seven Heads lay dead at the side of the pool.

And it is said that the people came running in their crowds to hear the glad news. Dancing and singing, it is said, blowing horns, beating drums, and clashing cymbals, they followed Koto Fananasia back to the pool. And when they saw the monster lying there dead, and knew that he would trouble them no more, it is said that such a roar of jubilation went up from them as never was heard on earth before. With sharp knives they ripped up the dead Monster's stomach, and dragged out the king's house and all the king's possessions: his gold and his silver, and his jewels, his embroidered sitting mats, and his velvet cushions, his coloured blankets and his polished weapons, his costly dishes and cooking pots, and his wine jars and his drinking cups.

So, one says, they set up the king's house in the place where it had been before. And the women fetched food, and the men opened the wine jars, and in the court in front of the king's house they all sat down to feast.

And they had not long been feasting, one says, when they heard a clatter of hoofs, and the King of the West and the Princess Minamina came riding into the courtyard. The two kings embraced, and the little princess kissed her father again and again. . . .

It is said that amid all this rejoicing King Amdriam Bahooka soon recovered his health and his spirits, and was never tired of boasting of how he alone, of all the kings on earth, had gone

down into a Monster's stomach and come out again, alive and hearty.

And Koto Fananasia, the faithful slave, one says, rejoiced to see his king happy; and never once reminded him, by word or look, of the frightened tears he had shed inside the Monster's stomach.

6 · King Josef

One day the good King Josef said to himself, 'Here I sit on my throne, surrounded by courtiers and flatterers – and what do I really know about the lives of my people? It is time I learned!'

So he disguised himself as a pilgrim, took a staff in his hand, and set out to wander on foot through his realm. Some people he found happy, some people he found unhappy; and some people he found kind and friendly, and some he found rough and rude. And as he journeyed he wrote down in a book that he carried the names of those whom he felt needed his help.

Towards evening he came into a village, and he was tired and hungry. So he knocked at the door of the first dwelling he came to; and that was a poor little hut, with one window downstairs and one window upstairs, and smoke curling from its one chimney.

Knock, knock, knock!

The door opened, and an old bent man looked out.

'Well now, who might you be?' said the old bent man. 'And what might you be wanting?'

'I am a traveller,' said the king. 'I have walked a long way, and I am tired and hungry. I should be grateful if I might come in and rest awhile.'

'Why surely, surely, come your ways in,' said the old man.

And he brought the king into a little kitchen, where an old woman was stooped over the fire.

'Wife,' says the old man, 'we have a visitor. We can spare him a bite?'

The old woman looked up and smiled. She had a pleasant wrinkled face. 'The potatoes will soon be cooked,' says she. 'And I am flavouring them with caraway to make them more tasty. But I have no meat to offer, for times are hard with us.'

'Hard indeed,' said the old man. 'I earn but a few pence cobbling shoes, and the missus earns but a few pence selling potatoes. As you see we are growing old, and we cannot labour as vigorously as we once did.'

'And have you no children to help you?' asked the king.

'Oh yes,' sighed the old man, 'we have three strong sons. But the king, bless his heart, called them into the royal army. It is long since we saw them.'

'And do they not write to you?'

'Write – why should they write? If they sent us letters we could not read them. But they are good lads, and do their duty by their country. One is in the cavalry, one in the artillery, and the third in the fusiliers. Eh dear, eh dear, we miss them sorely – but there, if the king has need of them, who are we to complain?'

'Now,' said the old woman, 'the potatoes are done to a turn. If you will be pleased to sit down at the table and eat?'

So they sat and ate. The king was very hungry. When the old woman asked him if the potatoes were to his liking, he said they were the best food he ever tasted. And having eaten and thanked the two old people, he got up to go on his way.

'What!' said the old man. 'Out in the dark at this time of night – and you not so young, after all! No, no, we've a blanket or two to spare, and you shall lay you down here in front of the fire, and sleep till morning.'

So, with a patched blanket under him, and a patched blanket over him, King Josef lay down and slept long and peacefully. When he woke in the morning the two old people were both busy: he bringing in logs for the fire, she setting the table with a loaf of bread and bowls of porridge, and more potatoes.

'The best breakfast ever I had in my life!' said the king, when
he had eaten. 'And will you tell me your name,' said he to the old
man, 'that I may remember it with gratitude?'

'Well now, Michael Breda is my name.'

'And the names of your three sons?'

'Wensel, and Karl, and Martin.'

The king wrote down these names, and the old woman watched
him and said, 'That looks pretty, that does, all those little
squiggles. But what comfort is there in squiggles or in names,
when those they belong to are far away?'

'They may yet come back to you,' said the king.

'And find us in our graves, most like,' said the old woman.

'Do you then grudge the king their service?' said King Josef.

'Oh no, no!' answered the old woman. 'I say bless the king, bless him, for I hear tell he is a good man. How should *he* know about our griefs?'

'It were well he *should* know,' said King Josef, as he bade the two old people goodbye.

So, after a day or two of more wandering, the king returned to his palace. And the first thing he did was to send for Wensel Breda – the old couple's eldest son.

Wensel was scared when he was told he must report to the king. He thought he must have done something wrong, though he couldn't imagine what that something could be. 'But there is nothing on my conscience,' he told himself. So head high and heart proud, he went into the king's presence and saluted smartly.

The king looked upon him kindly, and asked him where he came from. Wensel told him. And the king said, 'And are your parents still alive?'

'That I don't know, Royal Highness. They were already old when I left them.'

'And do you not write to them sometimes?'

'No, Royal Highness, I don't write. What would be the use? They can neither of them read.'

'And would you like to go home?'

'I should indeed, your highness. But there, why wish for the impossible?'

'It is not so impossible as you think,' said the king with a smile.

And he gave the astonished Wensel his discharge.

So off home went Wensel.

'Little father, little mother, I have my discharge. And here I am – a strong lad to work for you!'

Ah, what joy! What clapping of hands, what hugging and kissing!

The next day the king sent for Karl, the second son, and he too got his discharge and came home to the overjoyed old

69

couple. 'Little father, little mother, now you can rest. Here I am, another strong lad to work for you!'

And the day after that, King Josef sent for Martin, the youngest son.

'My lad, your two brothers have gone home. Is it your wish to follow them?'

'Oh, Royal Highness, I wish it with all my heart!' Martin was near to weeping for very joy.

'Well, you shall go,' said the king. 'Nor shall you go empty-handed. Here in this little bag are a hundred gold pieces. Tell your parents that this is in payment for a delicious supper and a warm bed and a delicious breakfast.'

So off went Martin. But when he gave his parents the king's message, they were aghast. The old woman shed tears: 'Such a poor supper, such a comfortless bed, such a mean breakfast – oh, oh, porridge and potatoes – and he *the king*!'

'Well now,' said the old man, 'didn't he praise the potatoes? Didn't he say they were the best food he ever tasted?'

'So he did, so he did!' cried the old woman. 'Here, give me that basket!'

'What now?' said the old man.

The old woman didn't answer. She was filling the basket full as it would hold with potatoes. And when the basket would hold no more, she slung it across her arm, and off with her to the palace, and insisting that she must see the king that minute, *that minute!*

'I doubt if he can see you,' said the lacquey at the door.

'Oh yes he can and he will!' said the old woman, 'for he is an angel of goodness, and 'tis Marta Breda says so.'

When the king was told who was asking for him, he had the old woman brought into him at once. And what did that old woman do but flop down and fling her arms about his knees. 'A hearty greeting, dear King Josef, from the happiest old woman in the world! And I've brought you some more potatoes, because you said they were the best food ever you tasted. I am only a silly old woman, but I love you with all my heart, dear King Josef. I give you a mother's blessing, praying that all may go well with you forever. Amen.'

And there she was, laughing and crying, and kissing his hands.

King Josef was so touched that he felt like laughing and crying himself. He had wine brought that they might drink each other's healths. And he gave the old woman another hundred gold pieces.

'Not in payment for the potatoes,' he explained, 'for they are beyond price – but just to remember me by.'

'As if I could ever forget you, dear Josef!' said she. 'Oh, ain't I a happy old woman! There's no old woman in the world happier than this old woman!'

And off she trotted home with her hundred gold pieces.

Well, well, you may be sure that these happenings were soon the talk of the town, and the story came to the ears of the mayor, who was a stupid, greedy fellow. 'Just fancy,' thought he, 'an old woman getting all that gold for a few miserable potatoes! What then would the king give for a really handsome present? It would be well to see into this! Let me consider! Why yes, of course, I have two beautiful thoroughbred colts – the very thing!'

So off went the mayor with his two colts to present to King Josef.

King Josef was in council, and could see no one. But he ordered the colts to be stabled, and the mayor to be given a well-locked little-chest, together with a letter saying that what the chest contained had cost him a great deal – namely three good soldiers and two hundred gold pieces.

The greedy mayor hurried off with his little chest. And when he got home he summoned a locksmith to open the chest.

'Go carefully, go very, very carefully!' said he to the locksmith. 'For the contents of this chest are precious, I tell you, yes precious!'

And indeed they were precious. What were they? Just the potatoes that the old woman had brought to the king. Nothing more.

7 · Vanooshka

Vanooshka lived with his father. His mother had been dead many years. One day his father said, 'Vanooshka, you are growing up, it is time you were taught a trade. We will go to the town and apprentice you to someone or other.'

So they set off. They went, they went, they went. They walked a long way. It began to rain.

Vanooshka said, 'Daddy, let us shelter here, under this fence.'

Behind the fence there was a big house, and in the house there lived an old, old man. He heard Vanooshka speaking and he called out, 'Who's there? What are you doing?'

'We are sheltering from the rain, I and my son,' said Vanooshka's father.

'Well, come in, come in,' shouted the old man. 'Don't stand there!'

And he opened the house door and let them in.

He looked at them. They were dripping wet. He bade them stand by the fire to dry themselves. He said. 'Where were you going?'

And Vanooshka's father answered, 'Where were we going? We were going to town to get my son taught a trade.'

The old man said, 'Give him to me for three years. I will teach him to know what is good and what is evil.'

'I should like to learn all about that,' said Vanooshka.

Well, they stayed the night with the old man. They got a

splendid supper, and splendid beds, and in the morning a splendid breakfast. And after breakfast Vanooshka's father took Vanooshka aside and said, 'My son, this old man is surely wise and pious. See that you obey him in all things.'

'Don't you worry about that, Daddy,' said Vanooshka. 'I'll obey him.'

So then Vanooshka's father went home.

And Vanooshka lived with the old man. He lived with him one year, he lived with him two years; but he didn't seem to be learning anything. So at the end of the two years he said, 'Grandaddy, I go in and out, I eat and I sleep, I drum with my fingers on the table, I hum a tune, I yawn or I laugh – and all these things I could do at home. Why don't you teach me a trade? If you are not going to teach me, I shall go home. But if you will teach me, I will stay.'

So then the old man gives Vanooshka the keys of six rooms and says, 'In these six rooms you will find people working at six different trades. And whichever trade you fancy, that one you shall learn.'

Vanooshka takes the keys. He unlocks the door of the first room. Now he is standing on the edge of the sea with a harbour wall behind him. On the sea, ships are coming and going; and in the harbour sailors are loading and unloading merchandise. What a cheerful bustle, what laughter, what singing and shouting! 'Yes, a sailor's life is a good life,' thinks Vanooshka.

But let's see what's in the other rooms.

Vanooshka unlocks the door of the second room. Well now, look – here's a flower garden – such a beautiful flower garden! The gardeners are busy, digging, hoeing, weeding, planting. There are roses and lilies, daffodils and pansies – every kind of flower. There are bees humming, and birds singing, and everywhere the scent of flowers. Vanooshka is touched to the heart. Ah, to live and work among such pretty, innocent things – that perhaps were best!

But we must look into the other rooms. Vanooshka unlocks

the third door. My word! Here are two armies fighting! Swords are flashing, cannon roaring, guns going bang, bang, bang! Vanooshka is so excited that he can't stand still, he's leaping up and down, he's doubling up his fists, he's yelling at the top of his voice. He wants to join in the battle, no matter on which side; he tries to snatch a sword from a soldier, but the soldier gives him a push: now he's outside the room again, and the door slams behind him. Vanooshka is panting – but to be a soldier, to fight in a noble cause, perhaps even to die an heroic death – is there on earth a better life?

However, there are three more doors to unlock.

Vanooshka unlocks the fourth door. Here are musicians, playing on many instruments – violins, guitars, harps, trumpets, harpsichords, bassoons, 'cellos, organs – oh the harmony, oh the music, joyous, solemn, soul-stirring, merry, sad! Vanooshka is in ecstasies, he is touched to the depths of his soul, he is actually shedding tears, tears of joy, tears of longing. He wipes away the tears with the back of his hand, tiptoes out of the room, shuts the door, and, passing on, unlocks the door of the fifth room.

Hullo, hullo, here are mountains! And along the tops of the mountains huntsmen in green coats are chasing deer. *Hilly-ho! Tally-ho! Ho, ho, ho!* Away they go, horses galloping, bugles blowing, stags running, dogs barking – oh, the clear bright air, the thrill, the wild excitement! 'If I had but a horse under me and were galloping with the rest,' thinks Vanooshka, 'what more on earth could I desire? Yes, yes, a huntsman's life for me! . . .'

And so to unlock the sixth door. Where are we now? In a little palace and such a little palace! Marble floors, golden pillars, silken curtains, velvet carpets, most elegant furniture, rooms beyond rooms, a banqueting hall, a dance hall, a musician's gallery, snug parlours, bedrooms in which kings might be proud to sleep. But not a king, nor a duke, nor a lord, nor a lady to be seen: only lacqueys in plum-coloured suits, moving about on silent feet. Ho, ho! If Grandaddy thinks to make Vanooshka a lacquey, he's mightily mistaken!

But what's this? A lacquey bowing low before Vanooshka, a lacquey ushering him into a long picture gallery, where the portraits of all the lords and ladies who have owned this palace hang on the walls. Some lords and ladies are wearing strange old-fashioned clothes: some lords with curly powdered wigs, some ladies with towering jewel-bedecked head-dresses . . . and so, as Vanooshka passes from one portrait to another, the clothes that the people are wearing become more and more familiar, and the faces too – now Vanooshka almost fancies he knows some of these people, for surely they are people of his father's time?

And so he comes to the last portrait of all. Ah ha, ah ha! Truly he knows *this* fellow – for it is a portrait of Vanooshka himself!

Well, well, well, if Grandaddy can make Vanooshka the owner of this palace, then pooh – a fig for all your trades!

So Vanooshka goes out and locks the sixth door behind him. Now he is going back to Grandaddy to tell him that he has decided to live like a prince in a palace.

But, see now, here's a seventh door, and this door like all the others is locked. But Vanooshka has only six keys – what's the meaning of that? Is there something in this seventh room that Grandaddy won't allow Vanooshka to see? Something perhaps better than anything he has yet seen? Vanooshka puts his ear against the door. He hears a murmur of voices, laughter and snatches of song. Girls' laughter, surely, girls' chatter, girls' singing. Vanooshka wants to see those girls; it is so long since he has spoken to anyone of his own age. He knocks gently. The laughter ceases, the voices are silent.

'*Please* let me in!' says Vanooshka.

No answer.

'*Why* won't you let me come in?' says Vanooshka.

No answer.

But there is a knot in the wood of the door, and Vanooshka has a jack-knife in his pocket. He works away with the jack-knife and cuts out the knot. Now he has made a hole, he has one eye

75

against the hole, he is peeping into the room. What does he see? He sees three girls seated there, embroidering tapestries with precious stones.

Vanooshka clears his throat, '*Hem, hem!*' The girls look up – ah, how pretty they are! One of them says, 'Is that you, Vanooshka? Why don't you come and visit us?'

'I want to come, but Grandaddy didn't give me the key to your room,' says Vanooshka.

'No, and he won't give it you,' says the second girl.

'But we'll tell you what to do,' says the third girl. 'When Grandaddy comes home this evening, give him a little glass of wine. Give him one little glass, and another little glass, and a third little glass. Then Grandaddy will fall asleep, and you can take the key. Ha! ha! It is a very little key, and he keeps it under his left moustache.'

Vanooshka went away. He waited; and in the evening the old man came home. He said, 'Vanooshka, did you take a look at the rooms?'

'Yes, Grandaddy.'

The old man said, 'You shall tell me about them tomorrow. Now I am tired and hungry.' He gave a rap on the table – there was supper: soup, meat, pudding. They sat down and ate. The old man was yawning. Vanooshka said, 'Grandaddy, I think a glass of wine would do you good.'

'Yes, Vanooshka, pour me out a glass.'

Vanooshka poured out a glass of wine.

The old man drank it up.

Vanooshka poured out another glass of wine.

The old man drank it up.

Vanooshka poured out a third glass of wine.

The old man drank it up. Now he was yawning and yawning. He said, 'Give me a hand to my bed, Vanooshka. Shake up the pillows, spread over me the sable fur coverings. . . .'

'All right, all right, Grandaddy, you lie down. I'll cover you up and make you cosy.'

The old man lies down. Vanooshka spreads the covers over him. Soon the old man is fast asleep.

But what a nuisance of an old man! He is lying on his left side! How can Vanooshka get the key from under his left moustache?

Vanooshka goes to the right hand side of the bed. He gives a tweak at the pillow. The old man mumbles something: he turns to pull the pillow straight. Now he is lying on his right side. Vanooshka holds his breath for a moment. The old man doesn't stir. Vanooshka takes the little key from under the old man's left moustache, tiptoes out of the room, and runs up to the room where the girls sit behind the locked door.

Now he unlocks the door, now he goes into the room. But he is feeling shy, he can't get out one word, he just stands there blinking.

The girls are laughing at him. 'What's the matter, Vanooshka, aren't we pretty?'

Vanooshka draws a long breath. 'You are – the prettiest – prettiest things in the whole world!'

'Well then, Vanooshka, over in that corner there is another door. Unlock it with your little key. It opens into another room. In that other room you will see, hanging on the wall, our lovely, jewel-bedecked, self-shining dance dresses. Bring them here, we will put them on, and you shall dance with us.'

Vanooshka unlocks the other door, he goes into the other little room, he takes the shining dresses off their pegs, he brings them to the girls. The girls put them on – my word, how those dresses glitter!

The girls begin to dance, they are holding out their hands to Vanooshka. 'Vanooshka, are we pretty?'

'I cannot look at you, you are so pretty.'

'Then dance with us, Vanooshka, dance with us!'

They take him by the hands. Now they are all whirling round together, fast, faster, faster. Vanooshka's head is spinning, he is laughing, the girls are laughing. . . . And then suddenly – how did it happen? – they all fall to the floor.

And the girls turn into bees, and fly out through the open window.

Oh, Vanooshka, what have you done? Oh, Vanooshka, what will the old man say? Vanooshka is stamping about, he is waving his arms, he feels he will go crazy. He rushes out of the room and goes back to the old man. The old man is still asleep. Vanooshka shouts, 'Wake up! Wake up!' He pulls the pillows from under the old man's head, he snatches up the sable fur coverings and flings them on the floor, shouting all the time, 'Wake up! Wake up!'

The old man wakes, he sits up, gives a tug at his left moustache. Yes, the key has gone. Now he knows what Vanooshka has been up to. 'So my grand-daughters have flown away, have they?' says he. 'I must go after them. It will take me three years to collect them. Bring me my clothes and my travelling cloak. You must wait here until I come back.'

The old man dressed and went away. And Vanooshka stayed alone in the house for three years.

He still had the keys of the six rooms. Sometimes he went into the first room, and helped the sailors load and unload the ships. Sometimes he went into the second room, and did a bit of digging in the garden. Sometimes he went into the fourth room. He found an old fiddle lying on a stool. He tried to play the fiddle and join in the orchestra, but the musicians turned him out. He went into the fifth room and climbed the mountains. But he had no horse – he couldn't join in the chase. He unlocked the door of the sixth room, and wandered through the little palace, went into the picture gallery, and shook his fist at his own portrait. 'Bah! What a fool you are! What an unhappy fool! . . .'

At the end of three years the old man came back, bringing the three girls with him. He said, 'Vanooshka, you have lived here for six years. Now you are of an age to get married. Which one of these girls will you have?'

'I will have the youngest,' said Vanooshka. 'But see, Grandaddy, I don't even know her name.'

'She is called Nadya,' said the old man.

So Vanooshka and Nadya were married. Vanooshka hoped they might now go and live in the little palace behind the sixth door. But not a bit of it! The old man gave them a small, quite ordinary house, near his own.

The old man put Nadya's self-shining dress in a casket, and brought the casket to Vanooshka. He said, 'Never let Nadya put on this dress. Can I trust you to keep it?'

'Oh yes, Grandaddy, I don't want my wife turning into a bee again! You can trust me!'

'Well, I hope I can,' said the old man.

Then came Sunday. Nadya said, 'I am going to church.' She dressed herself in black, and put on a dingy old shawl. She said, 'What a get up! I am like an old nun! If you were a good husband you would give me my self-shining dress. Then all the people would admire me. "Oh, oh," they would say, "what a pretty wife Vanooshka's got!"'

Vanooshka said, 'What do I care about other people? You are pretty enough for me, whatever you wear.'

No, he wouldn't give Nadya her self-shining dress. So she sat in church and sulked.

A week passed. Then the old man came to visit them. 'Well, Vanooshka, how are you getting on?'

'Thank you, Grandaddy, I'm getting on fine.'

'Well now, Vanooshka, you and Nadya must pay me a visit this afternoon. I have some guests coming for you to meet.'

'Thank you, Grandaddy, we'll come.'

So, early in the afternoon, Vanooshka said to Nadya, 'Come, get ready, we're going to meet Grandaddy's guests.'

Nadya went into the bedroom. She came out again in five minutes. She was wearing a brown dress and a black shawl. She said, 'See what a fright I am!' She went to the window, opened it and looked out. 'Here's a gold coach coming,' she said. 'It's bringing Grandaddy's guests.'

Vanooshka went to the window. He looked. The guests were getting out of the coach at the old man's gate. Silks, satins, velvets, broad hats, ostrich plumes, flowing cloaks, gold chains, jewels – you never saw such elegance! 'How can I face those people, and I looking like an old scarecrow?' said Nadya. 'No, I won't go! And I *am* so pretty, I *am* so pretty – it's a shame!'

And there she was, sobbing fit to break Vanooshka's heart.

Oh no, Vanooshka can't bear it! 'There, little wife, there, little dove, you shall have your pretty dress.' He hurries to fetch the casket, he unlocks it, he takes out the self-shining dress. 'There, little love, there little dove, put it on!'

Nadya claps her hands, laughs, flings off her black shawl and her old brown gown, puts on the self-shining dress. 'Am I pretty, Vanooshka, am I pretty now?' She kisses him. 'Well, let's go, Vanooshka, let's-*coo* now, *coo-roo* now, *coo-roo*. . . .'

Ah me, what's happened? Nadya has turned into a white dove. And the white dove flies out through the open window.

Vanooshka leaps out of the window after her. He falls to the ground, he jumps up, waving his arms, shouting. He doesn't know what he is doing, he begins to run, he runs and runs. He is not going to visit the old man. He is not going back into his house. He is going on and on: and if to the end of the world, well then to the end of the world – for he must, he *will* catch that white dove and bring her home.

So on he goes all day, running and walking, running and walking. In the evening he was crossing a moor, he was so tired he scarcely knew what he was doing, he stumbled into a boggy swamp, and sank up to his knees. See here, Grandaddy, how you have instructed Vanooshka! You have taught him what is good and what is bad, have you? Well, certainly he knows what is bad. It is bad to have lost his pretty wife; it is bad that he is up to his knees in a swamp; it is bad that he doesn't know how to get out!

And when, after panting and struggling, he at last gets out of the bog – well, it is still bad: for the sun has set, and it will soon be twilight, and then night – and where is Vanooshka? He is trudging along over the bleak moor, and his stomach is crying out for food, and he is so weary that he can scarce drag one foot after the other.

But Vanooshka came to the end of the moor at last. Now he was in a forest and he saw a little light among the trees. He went towards the light and came to a hut. He knocked on the door: no one answered. So he opened the door and went in.

A lighted candle set on a deal table, a fire burning brightly on the hearth. Vanooshka takes off his wet shoes and socks and his muddy trousers. He lies down beside the fire, yawns, falls asleep. . . .

Suddenly, from who knows where, comes the old witch, the Baba Yaga. As she runs, the forest crackles, the branches toss and bow, the leaves shower down. She bursts into the hut, she sees Vanooshka, she gnashes her teeth, now she will eat him, eat him, eat him. 'Ah ha! My supper!'

But Vanooshka wakes, he sits up, he scowls at the Baba Yaga. 'What are you about, you old witch? Is this the way old women behave in your country? You ought to say "Welcome, traveller!" You ought to heat the bath, wash me, comb the tangles from my hair, feed me, and ask "Where are you from, and how have you spent your life?" '

Well, well, here's a cheeky customer! But the Baba Yaga laughs, she likes his cheek, she heats water, she fills a bath tub, she washes Vanooshka, she wraps him in a rug, she hangs up his wet clothes to dry. She brews some broth, brings out a loaf of barley bread, says, 'Come eat. Tell me who you are, and where you have been living.'

'I have been living with grandfather, and he married me to his little grand-daughter, Nadya.'

'Well, well,' says the Baba Yaga, 'what a fool you are! That old man is my brother – you have married my little niece. Poor little dove, she flew through this forest some hours ago. I called to her but she wouldn't stop. Why did you give her the self-shining dress? She would have lived with you forever, if it wasn't for that dress.'

'Oh Auntie, Auntie, where is she now? And how can I find her? Tell me, tell me!'

'Well, all right – you must have patience with an old woman. Yes, I know where she is. But can you get to where she is?'

'Of course I can get to where she is! If she is on the earth I will walk and walk and walk until I reach her. If she is in Heaven I will climb up there. If she is in Hell, I will go down there, and not even Old Scritch, the biggest devil of them all, shall stop me!'

'Oh come, it's not as bad as that! Go to sleep now, and in the morning I will show you the way you must go.'

'As if I could sleep!' cried Vanooshka.

But sleep he did, and soundly.

Next morning he got a good breakfast. And whilst he was eating, the Baba Yaga cooked a big pancake. She put the pancake in a basket, and gave it to Vanooshka. Then she said, 'Come, it's time you were off' – and so led him out of the forest and up to the top of a high hill.

'Look yonder to the south,' says she. 'What do you see?'

'I see the flickering of a great fire.'

'It is not the flickering of a fire,' says the Baba Yaga. 'It is the gleaming of the sun on the golden palace of the hard-hearted enchantress, Queen Glafyra, who now holds our little dove, our poor little Nadya, captive. Maybe you will be able to set our Nadya free, maybe you won't. I can't see into the future as far as that. I can only tell you how to get into Queen Glafyra's palace.

'At the palace gate you will find three lions crouching. They will want to leap upon you and devour you, but you will break the pancake into three pieces and give them a piece each. Then, whilst they are eating their pancake, you can slip past them, and cross the courtyard. At the entrance door to the palace three sentries stand on guard. They won't want to let you pass. But you will hit one of them so hard that he flies off his feet and topples over the next one. Then the third will say, "Walk up, walk up". And you will walk up. You will come into one room, you will pass into a second room, and so into a third. And in

82

this third room you will find the enchantress, Queen Glafyra, seated on a golden throne. She will ask you who you are, and why you have come, and you will tell her. After that – heaven help you! – for I cannot.'

Then the Baba Yaga took two little bones out of her pocket. One was a raven's little bone, the other was a pike's little bone. She gave the bones to Vanooshka. 'Keep these carefully,' said she, 'for I think they may come in useful. . . . And now be off with you.'

And she gave Vanooshka such a prod in the back as sent him running down the hill.

So, running and walking, running and walking, he travelled for many miles, and came at last to the golden palace of the enchantress, Queen Glafyra. Before the palace gate lay three lions. When these lions saw Vanooshka they sprang up, they roared, they were about to pounce upon him and tear him to bits, but he thrust into each of their open jaws a piece of the pancake the Baba Yaga had given him; and they wagged their tails like friendly dogs, and let him pass.

Now he is hurrying across the palace courtyard, now he comes to a flight of golden steps leading to the great entrance door of the palace. At the bottom of the steps stand two sentries, guns at shoulders. The sentries lower their guns. No, they don't intend to let Vanooshka pass. But Vanooshka doubles up his fist, he gives one sentry such a blow that he flies off his feet and topples over the other. Vanooshka runs up the steps. At the top of the steps stands another sentry. But this one is bowing, he is opening the door, he is saying, 'Enter, my lord, enter!' Ha! What a coward!

Vanooshka goes into the palace. He goes through one room, he goes through a second room, he goes into a third room. In this third room the enchantress, Queen Glafyra — black-haired, dark-eyed, majestic, wonderful to behold — sits on a golden throne.

'Ha, Vanooshka, what brings you here?'

'What brings me here indeed? I have come to fetch my darling wife, my darling Nadya.'

'But if I do not choose to give you your wife, Vanooshka, what then?'

'What then? I will scream the place down! I will thrust my fist into your cruel eyes! I will tear the heart out of your evil body!'

Queen Glafyra laughs. 'Your little tantrums are very amusing, Vanooshka. Come, I will make a bargain with you. Try if you can hide from me. If I cannot find you, I will set your Nadya free (I have the little dove here in a cage). But if I find you, then I am afraid you must lose your head. I will give you three tries. Now don't stand glaring at me — be off and hide yourself.'

Vanooshka turns on his heel. He goes out of the throne room. Where shall he hide? He wanders out of the palace into a small bushy meadow. 'Shall I creep under a bush?' thinks he. 'Bah! She will set her dogs sniffing here, there, everywhere.' He looks about him, he puts his hand in his pocket, he feels there the raven's little bone that the Baba Yaga has given him. He takes it out, flings it down.

Suddenly — from who knows where? — comes flying an enormous raven. 'What do you want of me, Vanooshka?'

'Raven, Raven hide me,
So that Glafyra shan't find me!'

Raven takes Vanooshka under the arms, he drags him away into a boggy swamp, he pushes Vanooshka down into the swamp. Now only Vanooshka's head is showing above the swamp. Raven perches on Vanooshka's head and spreads his wings over it. . . .

Queen Glafyra steps from her throne. She rings a silver bell. *Tinkle, tinkle, tinkle!* Servants come hurrying.

'Servants, bring me my little magic looking glass, in which the whole world, and everything that is in the world, can be clearly seen.'

The servants bring the looking glass. Queen Glafyra looks

into it, turns it this way and that way. 'Now I will find Vanooshka!' She searches everywhere, along the meadows, through the forests, and into the depths of the sea. No, he isn't in any of these places. She turns the looking glass on the boggy swamp: there sits Raven — and what is that just showing from under Raven's outspread wings? What indeed but a lock of Vanooshka's curly hair.

'Raven, pull Vanooshka out of the swamp, and bring him here.'

Raven snatches Vanooshka out of the swamp, carries him to the sea, dips him in and washes the mud off him, fans him dry with his wings, and brings him to Queen Glafyra.

'Ah, Vanooshka, that was clever, but not clever enough! Now go and hide again.'

Vanooshka goes out, he goes to stand by the sea. He takes from his pocket the pike's little bone that the Baba Yaga had given him. He throws down the bone. Then there comes swimming a mighty pike.

'Pike, Pike, hide me,
So that Glafyra shan't find me.'

Pike takes Vanooshka in his mouth. He dives down to the bottom of the sea and creeps under a great stone. He swallows Vanooshka. But Vanooshka is too big for Pike to swallow entirely: the toe of one of Vanooshka's boots is sticking out of Pike's mouth.

Queen Glafyra looks in her magic glass. She turns it this way, that way: up to the heavens, through the forests, along the meadows, down to the sea. Ah ha, ah ha! What is that down at the bottom of the sea? Isn't that the toe of Vanooshka's boot, sticking out of Pike's mouth?

'Servants,' cries Glafyra, 'Come here! Just look, just look where Vanooshka has hidden himself!'

The servants come running, they look in the mirror, they laugh.

'Pike, Pike,' calls Queen Glafyra, 'toss up Vanooshka on to dry land.'

Pike rises from the sea bed, he spits Vanooshka out on to dry land. What a sight Vanooshka looks! Everything on him is crumpled, and there are bits of seaweed all over him. He bursts into tears. He comes to the palace. The servants are laughing at him. But they dry him off, and give him a new suit of clothes.

'Now, Vanooshka,' says Queen Glafyra, 'it is growing late. You can eat and go to bed. Tomorrow morning you shall hide from me for the last time.'

How can Vanooshka eat, how can Vanooshka sleep? He gulps down a glass of wine, and goes to lie down in the bed which the servants have prepared for him. No, he can't even close his eyes; he lies and stares at the darkness.

'Vanooshka, Vanooshka!' A voice calling very, very softly. Oh, Vanooshka knows that voice — it is the voice of his darling Nadya.

'Where are you?' he whispers.

'Open the door, Vanooshka.'

Vanooshka opens the door. Who flies in? The little white dove, his darling Nadya. She has torn her way out of her cage, and her little breast is bleeding. 'Vanooshka, don't despair. Vanooshka, keep up your heart! I will tell you where to hide.'

Then she whispers in his ear, flutters out of the room, and goes back into her cage. . . .

In the morning, there is Queen Glafyra seated on her golden throne. And there is Vanooshka standing before her.

'Good morning, Queen Glafyra.'

'Good morning, Vanooshka. You look happy today.'

'Queen, I am feeling happy.'

'And yet today you must lose your head, Vanooshka.'

'That is as God wills, your majesty.'

'Well, be off and hide for the last time.'

Vanooshka walks away proudly. He goes into a empty room, where there is a large mirror. The mirror is framed in silver, it reaches from floor to ceiling, and it stands out a foot or two from the wall. Vanooshka squeezes himself in behind the mirror. Now he is standing between the mirror and the wall.

Queen Glafyra rises from her throne. She rings her silver bell. *Tinkle, tinkle, tinkle*! Servants come hurrying.

'Servants, bring me my little magic looking glass.'

The servants bring the little magic looking glass. Queen Glafyra looks into it, turns it this way and that way. She turns it up to the heavens: Vanooshka is not there. She turns it on the earth, she looks through the forests, along the meadows, along the sea shore, and down through the depths of ocean: Vanooshka is in none of these places. Where can he be? Well, perhaps he is hiding in the palace? Queen Glafyra gets down from her throne, walks about the room, flings open the door, stands in the corridor, turning the little magic looking glass this way and that way. She looks into every room, through all the state apartments, along every corridor, into the kitchens, down through all the cellars, up into all the attics, she comes into the room where Vanooshka stands behind the wall mirror.

Vanooshka is holding his breath. Queen Glafyra is staring into the wall mirror. She sees only herself; and what she sees does not please her.

'Bah! How ugly I am looking this morning!'

She stamps her foot, she feels like screaming, for an hour or more she is searching, but at last she gives up. 'Very well, Vannoshka, you win! Come out of your hiding place!'

But Vanooshka doesn't stir.

'Vanooshka, come, come! You have beaten me, your life is safe!'

Vanooshka doesn't stir.

'Vanooshka, come! Vanooshka, come! I have promised you your life — what more do you want?'

Vanooshka doesn't stir.

'Vanooshka, a queen does not go back on her word. Did I promise you your little dove, your darling Nadya? Very well, you shall have her. See, I am opening the dove's cage, see I am setting your little dove free, see I have turned her back into her true shape, see she stands here at my side! Call him, Nadya, call this tiresome Vanooshka, tell him the game is up, tell him he has beaten me, tell him to come here!'

Truly the white dove has fluttered out of her cage. At a touch of Queen Glafyra's hand, the white dove has turned back into Nadya. Nadya stands at the queen's side and laughs. 'Vanooshka,' she calls in her soft little voice, 'you can come out now, you are safe!'

Vanooshka steps out from behind the mirror. He runs to hug his darling Nadya. Queen Glafyra grinds her teeth with rage. 'Go, go,' she screams, 'get out of my sight, both of you!'

So hand in hand Vanooshka and Nadya go out of the queen's gleaming golden palace. Hand in hand they travel back towards home, mile after mile: over the moors, through the forests, across the plains; and come at last to where Grandaddy's big house stands behind its wooden fence.

And see, there is old man Grandaddy, hurrying to open the front door.

'Welcome home, my children! And you, Vanooshka, what was it I said I would teach you when you first came to me?'

'You said, Grandaddy, that you would teach me to know what is good and what is evil.'

'And have you learned that lesson, Vanooshka?'

'Yes, Grandaddy, I think I have.'

'Then here is the key of the sixth door, Vanooshka. Your little palace is waiting for you.'

Vanooshka and Nadya go to live in the little palace. And Vanooshka's father comes to live with them.

Now here is Vanooshka proudly showing his father all over the palace. Last of all they come to the picture gallery. Vanooshka's father goes from portrait to portrait. 'I don't seem to recognise many of these people,' he says.

Vanooshka says, 'At least you will recognise the fellow in the last portrait of all, for that is myself.'

But the picture of Vanooshka is not now the last of the portraits. Beyond the picture of Vanooshka is a picture of Nadya.

In the picture she is sitting under a cherry tree in a garden. Two handsome little boys are standing, one on either side of her. And in her lap sits a beautiful baby girl.

When Vanooshka saw that picture he laughed for joy and said, 'What a knowledgeable old fellow is Grandaddy! Many a one knows the things that have been, and most of us know the things that now are; but only people like Grandaddy know the things that are to come.'

8 · The Two Enemy Kings

King Fritz and King Jochem ruled over neighbouring kingdoms. King Fritz was a good man, but somewhat stupid. King Jochem was a bad man — in fact he was a wicked wizard — and he hated King Fritz.

Now King Fritz's wife, the beautiful Queen Ilsabel, was expecting her first baby. And King Fritz was so excited about this that he couldn't stay still; he kept dashing about the palace and getting on every one's nerves. So Queen Ilsabel said, 'Dear husband, why must you stay indoors on such a fine morning? Since you have no business to attend to, why not order out your horse, summon a page or two to accompany you, and go for a ride through the forest?'

'Yes,' said King Fritz, 'I will go for a ride — but I will go alone. Why should anyone accompany me?'

'Then all I beg and pray is that you will keep away from the frontier,' said Queen Ilsabel; 'for you know how our neighbour, King Jochem, is always lying in wait to do you a mischief.'

'Pah!' said King Fritz. 'A fig for old Jochem!'

And his horse being brought round, saddled and bridled, off he rode.

'*Tra la la! Tra la la!*' King Fritz was singing as he rode, not very tunefully it must be owned, but very joyfully. He was so happy, so happy! He was so looking forward to having a little son and heir — or would it be a little daughter? Well, with whichever the good God sent, King Fritz would be delighted.

But the day was hot, and what with galloping and singing, and being so excited, King Fritz was thirsty. A drink of water he must have, yes he really must have! Now he was slowing down and looking this way and that way for a spring or well. But he couldn't find a spring, and he couldn't find a well, and he grew thirstier and thirstier. . . .

Hullo! Someone coming this way: a man walking towards him, a man who wore high rubber boots, a lean man who carried a ladder over his shoulder, and a spade in his hand.

King Fritz pulled up his horse. 'Good morrow, my friend.'

'Good morrow to you, my lord King.'

'Good friend, where have you come from, and why are you walking about in those high boots on this fine morning?'

'My lord King, I wear high boots to keep my feet and legs dry. I am a well-maker, and I have just been digging out a well close by.'

'Ah!' cried King Fritz, quite overjoyed. 'Lead me to that well that I may drink, for I am parched with thirst!'

'If your honour would condescend to dismount and come this way — it is but a step or two through these trees.'

So King Fritz jumped off his horse, and followed the well-digger down a little path among the trees.

In two minutes they came to the well — a deep, deep well.

'Owing to the drought the water is somewhat far down,' said the well-digger; 'and I have not yet had time to fix up the buckets and the windlass. But you see there is a rope ladder here — if your majesty would deign to descend.'

King Fritz didn't need urging. He was scrambling down the ladder into the well all in a moment. Now he was dipping up the clear bright water with his hands, now he was drinking — ah, how refreshing, how good and pure the water!

Over the edge of the well the lean man was watching, the lean man's eyes were glinting, the lean man's mouth was twisted into an evil smile. King Fritz, looking up, saw that face for one moment . . . the next moment all was darkness, for the lean man had heaved a great stone slab over the top of the well.

Yes, King Fritz was caught like a rat in a trap.

'Open up, open up this instant!' he shouted indignantly. 'How dare you play tricks on me! I am the king of this country!'

'Of this country?' laughed the well-digger. 'Oh no, King Fritz. You have stepped over the border into *my* country. I am your neighbour, King Jochem. I have long been waiting to catch you — and now I've got you! What will you give me to set you free?'

'I will give you as much gold and silver as four horses can carry,' cried King Fritz.

'Pah! What do I want with your gold and silver?' sneered King Jochem. 'I have enough of my own. But I hear that your good wife, Queen Ilsabel, is expecting a baby. If she gives birth to a son, and if you will promise to give me that son as soon as he is eighteen years old, I will set you free.'

'No, no, I cannot do that!' cried King Fritz.

'Then stay where you are and rot!' snarled King Jochem.

So for a long time King Fritz was down there at the bottom of the well, begging, imploring, and threatening by turns. And King Jochem was standing on the well-cover, mocking and sneering. But when King Fritz thought of his dear queen Ilsabel, and how she would grieve, and how she would send out messengers searching here, searching there, and of how those messengers could never find him, and how, after all, the baby might be a girl, and everything would come right — ah, then at last King Fritz called up, 'So be it, if I must I must — and may the good God punish you as you deserve!'

'I'll take my chances about that!' laughed King Jochem.

Then he lifted the cover off the well, and King Fritz climbed out.

'Now if you will just sign this paper,' said King Jochem. 'You see I have written out our agreement very fairly.'

King Fritz looked at the paper. Oh, the hateful, hateful words.

If my queen Ilsabel should bear me a son, I, King Fritz, hereby take my oath to hand over this son on his eighteenth birthday to my esteemed enemy, King Jochem.

So, having signed the paper and handed it back to King Jochem, King Fritz got on his horse and rode sadly home, hearing behind him the loud laughter of his enemy.

But, as he neared home, other sounds greeted his ears: the merry clamour of church bells, and the huzzas of his people as they thronged the open space before the palace. 'Our queen has borne a son, our queen has given us an heir to the throne! God bless our lovely queen, and our little prince, and our good king, Fritz!'

What could King Fritz do but pretend to rejoice with his people? But in his heart he wept. And when, by and by, he told his queen the sad story, she wept with him. However, she said he could have done no other. And that comforted him a little.

The little prince was christened Otto, and certainly he was a fine lad, strong, handsome, good tempered, and brave. Everyone loved him. As to the king and queen, they doted on him. It was as if they were trying to make the most of a treasure that they must presently part with; and if they did not thoroughly spoil him, that was not to their credit, but to his.

It was Queen Ilsabel who, on Otto's eighteenth birthday, drew him aside, and with many tears told him of the tragic fate that awaited him.

'But do not — oh, do not blame your father,' said she. 'What else could he do?'

'No, I don't blame him,' answered Otto. 'But it seems that what the father has sown, the son must reap.' And then and there he slung a knapsack over his shoulder, and walked away to meet his fate.

So, after he had been walking many hours he came into a forest, and there he saw an old, old man, sitting on a fallen tree stump.

'Good day, Prince Otto,' said the old, old man.

'Good day to you, little old one,' said Otto. 'How comes it that you know my name?'

'I know many things,' said the old, old man. 'I know where you are going, and why you are going. And I can give you some good advice if you will take it from me.'

'I am glad to take advice from all who can give it,' said Otto.

'Well then,' said the old, old man, 'when you come out of the forest, you will find yourself on an eight mile long straight road, which is bordered on both sides by poplar trees, and leads direct to King Jochem's palace. Now, as you value your life, pick up every branch that falls down from those trees whilst you are walking along the road. You will hear a voice telling you to give back the branches, but pay no heed. Let the voice plead, let it threaten, let it say what it will, just you hold on to those branches, until you hear the voice saying, 'Prince Otto, in the name of heaven and of all good, give me my hands!' Then lay the branches down, and go on your way.'

'That is strange advice you are giving me,' said Otto.

'And strange are the happenings that await you,' said the old man. 'But a stout heart will carry the possessor of it safely through many perils.'

So having spoken, the old man vanished. First he was there; then he was not there. And Prince Otto walked on, greatly wondering.

Well, it wasn't long before he reached the end of the forest; and sure enough, before him stretched the eight mile long flat road, bordered by poplar trees, just as the old man had said. But there was not a breath of wind, not a leaf stirred, the poplar trees stood up straight and motionless, pointing skyward — how should any branches fall in such a calm? So Otto walked on for about a mile, hearing no sound at all, except the light sound of his own footsteps.

And then, suddenly, with a flash of lightning and a blast of thunder, came the storm: the wind roared, the tall poplars rocked and bowed, and with a crashing and a tearing and a confusion of whirling leaves, down fell their branches on to the road. One branch fell at Otto's feet, he picked it up, and walked on: down fell another branch at Otto's feet, he picked it up, and walked on. Down fell another branch and yet another, and as Otto picked them up, he heard a voice crying from out of the trees, 'Give me back my hands! Give me back my hands!'

But Otto paid no heed; he walked on, picking up the branches as they fell until he was almost bent double under the weight of them. And then, just as he was beginning to feel that it would be impossible for him to pick up and carry one more branch, a voice, strong and clear as the voice of a trumpet, yet of remarkable sweetness called from above his head, 'Prince Otto, in the name of heaven and of all good, give me my hands!'

And most gratefully Otto obeyed that voice, laid down his burden of branches at the side of the road, and walked on his way.

So he came to the end of the long road, and now before him flowed a broad, fast-rushing river. Over the river stretched a bridge, and on the other side of the bridge rose the great walls and gilded pinnacles of a palace — the palace of the wizard king, Jochem.

'So I have arrived at last,' thought Otto, and stepped on to the bridge. What happened? The bridge gave a heave, and flung him off into the river. Down he went under the water, and up he came spluttering and striking out for land. But the rushing waters seized upon him, tossing him here, tossing him there, dragging him down into the depths, flinging him up again . . . and down again, and up again. As if he had been a helpless babe, so the waters played with him, until his arms grew weak, and his breath left him. 'This is the end,' thought Otto, as he sank once more under the raging water. . . .

But it was not the end. Someone's arms were round him, someone was lifting his head above water, someone, with one arm supporting him, was swimming strongly, bringing him to land outside the palace gates, chafing his numbed hands and feet, wringing the water out of his sodden clothes, assuring him that he had only to do all that she bade him, and everything would yet go well.

Yes, it was a maiden who had brought him ashore. And Otto, as he sat up and gazed into her face, thought that never had he dreamed or imagined that a maiden could be so beautiful.

'Who are you?' he asked.

'I am King Jochem's adopted daughter,' said the maiden, 'stolen from my home before I could speak or walk. Some of his magic I have learned from him, and with all my heart and soul I try to turn his evil into good. Now I will leave you, for we must not be seen together. But rest assured that all I can do to protect you, I will do.'

Then the maiden walked away from him, and Otto went into the palace, announced his name, and was brought with all speed into a small room, where King Jochem sat on a three legged stool, drumming his fingers on a wooden table.

There was nothing kingly about this Jochem. Tousle-headed, beady-eyed, lean and scraggy, and yet, and yet — there was something about him that made Otto shudder: as if he stood in the presence of all the wickedness of the world. And Jochem's smile, as he rose to greet Otto, was such a smile as one might expect to see on the face of Satan himself.

'Ah, so you have come at last!' said King Jochem. 'I have been expecting you with impatience. I was afraid my river might have forestalled me in the pleasure of making your acquaintance. A heartfelt pleasure, I assure you, though a brief one. But you must be tired after your long journey, so today you shall rest. To-morrow we will try your mettle. I will give you a horse to ride. If you can master that horse — good. If not, I regret to tell you that the faggots are already heaped about your funeral pyre. But it will be a princely blaze, a royal spectacle, I promise you. And I myself and all my court will be in attendance to grace the show.'

So, with many an evil grin, King Jochem summoned a young page, who led Otto to a room where a good meal was spread for him. Otto, soaked to the skin from his tumble into the river, was

by this time shivering with cold. But the page, a pleasant enough little fellow, helped him off with his wet clothes, wrapped him in a robe of softest swansdown, and after he had eaten, showed him into a bedroom where a bright fire blazed merrily on the hearth, and the rays of the setting sun, shining through the window, cast a radiance on the opposite wall.

But how could Otto sleep? He didn't even attempt to get into bed. He sat and watched the sun go down, thought of King Jochem's evil grin, and wondered what the morrow had in store for him. To ride a horse . . . well, that seemed no difficult task; Otto was a good rider . . . and yet, and yet — it was certain that King Jochem's evil grin boded him no good . . . .

Twilight. Night. The sky a-glitter with stars, the room in darkness, and Otto still sitting at the window, thinking puzzled thoughts, when the door opened noiselessly, and someone stepped into the room. Otto swung round, leaped to his feet, clapped a hand to the dagger at his belt — if he was now to be murdered it should not be without a fight!

But a gentle voice whispered 'Hush!' And by the light of the shaded lamp that she carried, Otto saw that it was the maiden who had saved him from drowning in the river. 'Prince,' she said, 'I know the task that King Jochem has set you, and although it may sound an easy one, I assure you that it is not so. And I have come to help you as best I can.'

Then the maiden took a book from under her arm, sat down at a table, opened the book, and began to read. And no sooner had she read one sentence than a silvery-shining ghostlike being stepped into the room. And as she read on, there appeared another shining ghostlike being, and yet another, and another. And when twenty of these strange beings stood before her, the maiden gave them her orders.

'Four of you will hold the horse that Prince Otto is to ride,' she said, 'four and four will stand on either side of it, four will stand behind it, and four will help the prince to mount. And when he is mounted, by ten and by ten you will hedge the way

99

to the courtyard gate, so that the animal must go straight forward. That is the command I lay upon you. Do you understand, and will you faithfully fulfil it?'

'We understand your command, and we will faithfully fulfil it,' answered the ghostlike beings. Then one by one their shapes grew dimmer and dimmer, until one by one they had faded into nothingness.

The maiden shut her magic book. 'Now some advice for you, prince,' she said 'The animal that King Jochem will give you to ride is in truth no horse, but one of King Jochem's devil servants in disguise. Therefore, as King Jochem would be merciless to you, do you be merciless with his servant. Ride him with whip and spur, do not let him carry you whither he will, but direct his course towards the sandhills outside the city. On the sandhills gallop him up and down, up and down, until the brown horse becomes a white horse from the foam that covers him. Then he will be tamed, and you can ride him back to the palace. . . . Now I will leave you. Sleep in peace, Prince Otto.'

Then the maiden, taking up her book and her lamp, went quietly away. And Otto got into bed.

Almost immediately he fell into a dreamless sleep, and didn't wake until the young page came to call him in the morning, bringing his clothes, dried and pressed, helping him to bath and dress, and with the utmost respect and kindness ushering him into the room where he had supped last night, and where now breakfast was awaiting him.

Breakfast over, a smirking valet came in to announce that King Jochem requested the pleasure of Prince Otto's attendance in the palace courtyard; and Otto went out to find King Jochem seated in state, wearing his crown and royal robes, and surrounded by a throng of court officials, but looking, for all his grandeur, more mean and sly than he had looked the day before, when perched on the three legged stool.

'Ah, good morning, good morning, dear prince,' said King Jochem, twisting lips into an evil grin. 'I hope you found yourself well served, and have spent a peaceful night? You did not by any chance dream of funeral pyres and flaming faggots?'

Otto bowed politely. 'Thank you,' he said, 'I was excellently served. I slept well, and I do not remember that I dreamed at all.'

'And you are looking forward to your ride?' said King Jochem.

'Very much,' said Otto.

'Then bring out the horse!' cried King Jochem.

At once two grooms appeared, leading a brown horse, whose head drooped and whose knees trembled.

'Is this my mount?' cried Otto, feeling truly insulted.

'That is your mount,' grinned King Jochem. 'You will find him more spirited than you expect.'

And indeed, no sooner did Otto lay his hand on the bridle, than the horse reared and struck out savagely with his fore feet, plunging this way and that way, setting back his ears, rolling his eyes wickedly, baring his teeth, snapping at Otto's arm, and all but flinging Otto to the ground.

But at that instant, all unseen to the assembled crowd but visible to Otto, came the maiden's ghost servants. Four of the ghosts caught the horse by the bridle, four closed in on either side of the horse, four stood behind it, and four swiftly lifted Prince Otto into the saddle. And then, once Otto was mounted, by ten and by ten the ghosts ranged themselves in two lines, hedging the way to the courtyard gate, so that the horse could gallop no way but through that gate. And through that gate he went, galloping at such a furious pace, plunging and kicking so wildly, that it was all Otto could do to keep his seat in the saddle.

Wilfully now that horse would make his way downwards to the river, but the ghosts barred that way, and Otto, with triumphant shouts, headed him towards a range of sandhills, and over those sandhills galloped him up and down, up and down, for one hour, for two hours, for three hours, until from a brown horse he became a white horse from the foam that covered him. Then Otto turned and rode him back to the palace, as meek a creature as ever man mounted.

The palace courtyard was empty when Otto rode into it; but startled faces peered from windows, and very soon King Jochem came hurrying, with rage and disappointment in his heart, but with his ugly mouth twisted into a would-be friendly grin.

'You have done well, my prince,' said he, as Otto slid down from the horse's back. 'The rest of the day is at your own disposal. But your funeral pyre still waits, and tomorrow we will give your horsemanship another trial.'

Then, with a smile that was by no means friendly, King Jochem turned on his heel; a groom led the exhausted horse back to the stable, and Otto went into the palace to find the maiden waiting for him in the little room where he had break-fasted.

The maiden was laughing. 'So,' said she, 'you have mastered the brown horse, Prince Otto. But do you know what horse it is that you have so severely punished? That brown horse was no other than King Jochem's treasurer, who now lies in bed, poor fellow, with sticking plaster all over him, and doubtless cursing his unfeeling master, who forced such a humiliating role upon him. Tomorrow the king's prime minister will play his part, in the shape of a dapple grey; but my ghosts will be in attendance to see you safely mounted, and your own good horsemanship will set that dapple galloping over the sandhills without stay, until the dapple grey horse becomes a white horse from the foam that covers him, and you will ride a sad and sorry steed back to the palace. Then there will be another of King Jochem's ministers lying in his bed, poor fellow, with sticking plaster all over him, moaning and groaning and cursing his unfeeling master. . . . But here is food and drink spread ready for you. And when you have eaten we will wander out into the palace gardens and speak to each other of our hopes and fears, and all the secrets of our hearts.'

Who now was happy but Prince Otto? Let tomorrow bring

what it would, today was all gladness. Before the day was out, he had told the maiden of his love for her, and she had agreed that if they could escape in safety, she would return with him to his father's kingdom, and become his wife.

In this happy mood he spent the rest of the day; in this happy mood went to his bed and slept soundly; in the same happy mood rose next morning, and having breakfasted, went out into the palace courtyard, where King Jochem again was enthroned, and looking even uglier and more venomous than the day before.

Nor did King Jochem waste any time this morning in pretty speeches. He immediately called for the dapple grey to be brought out, and out that horse came, rearing and plunging and kicking at the grooms who led it. But the maiden's faithful ghosts were in attendance; they closed in upon the furious animal, and whether it stood on its hind legs, or flung those hind legs high into the air, the ghosts had Prince Otto safely up in the saddle, and by ten and by ten hedging the way on either side, they saw Prince Otto through the courtyard gate, and galloping towards the sandhills.

What a gallop! What kicking and plunging and wild careering! What flinging up of heels and down of head, what sideways leaps, what abrupt stops, what sudden determination to lie down and roll! But with whip and spur Prince Otto drove him on, and by and by with heaving flanks and drooping head, and body covered with foam, the horse gives up the struggle: he becomes docile as an old sheep, and Otto turns his head and rides him home.

That evening it was King Jochem's prime minister who lay plastered and bandaged, moaning in his bed, whilst the maiden supped with Otto, and spoke quietly of the morrow.

'It will be a black horse for you to ride tomorrow,' she said, 'and that black horse will be far fiercer and wilder than either the brown or the dapple, for it will be none other than King Jochem himself, and with more ferocity than any wild beast he will attempt to unhorse and trample you. But my ghosts will see you mounted and heading for the sandhills, and if you can but keep your seat and ride him hard, until from a black horse he becomes a white horse from the foam that covers him — why then, dear Otto, the victory is ours, and after that —'

'And after that?' said Otto.

'Heaven help me, I can see no farther into the future,' said the maiden. 'But I think we must somehow make our escape. . . .'

Next morning, when Otto went out prepared for his ride, he found only a grinning stable master to receive him. The stable master told him with many winks and grimaces that King Otto had gone to see to the funeral pyre. 'Which is to be lit later on today,' said the stable master, 'after the black has thrown you. Though of course if the black should trample you to death, we should all regret it; but I don't think he will, no I don't think he will, he is a sympathetic animal, he won't like to disappoint us with the burning of a dead body, which after all would be but a sorry spectacle, when compared to the burning of a living one.'

'Will you kindly stop your chatter and bring out the horse,' said Otto curtly.

'So I will, so I will,' said the grinning stable master. 'He is making a shambles of his stall at this minute in his eagerness to serve you.'

And he hurried off to the stables, and soon came out again, leading a magnificent black stallion, who held his head high and walked with a proud step as if he owned the world.

'If it is really you, King Jochem,' thought Otto in admiration, 'you make a far finer animal than ever you make a man. But come now,' said he, putting a foot in the stirrup, 'let us try your paces!'

Now before and behind and on either side, the maiden's ghosts were in attendance; but the stallion stood quite quietly for Otto to mount, and quietly, too, trotted out through the courtyard gates, and headed for the sandhills.

'Why this is child's play!' thought Otto. 'What can it mean?'

And then suddenly he seemed to hear the maiden's voice

whispering 'Oh, beware, beware!' And at that instant the stallion gave a leap, and with a downward fling of his head and an upward fling of his hind legs had Otto off the saddle, and hanging head downward, with his right foot out of the stirrup, and his hands clutching wildly at the stallion's legs.

Now the animal was off at a furious gallop, now he was kicking, now he was leaping, now he was up on his hind legs, now he was down on his front legs with his hind legs in the air, and an upside-down Otto, with one foot still caught in the stirrup, was being dragged along like any old sack, thumping and bumping over the whirling sand.

'This is the end!' thought Otto. 'Oh my maiden, my maiden, whom I shall never see again!'

And even as he thought this thought, kind hands (could it be the maiden's own hands?) lifted him up into the saddle again; and with no more thought of child's play, but with tightened rein and lashing whip, Otto was urging the stallion into a furious gallop, and shouting in the triumph of his heart.

Up and down the little range of hills, with the sand hissing under the stallion's hoofs and rising in whirling clouds to blind the eyes of both horse and rider, they went at that furious gallop, hour after hour: until the stallion, white with foam and drawing his breath in gasps, slackened his pace. Now his head drooped, now his feet stumbled, and still Otto lashed him with the whip and urged him on . . . and rode him back to the palace at last — a humbled, staggering animal with all the spirit gone from him.

'And if I didn't know who you really are,' said Otto, as he slid off the stallion's back, 'I should be ashamed of the way I have treated you!' And leaving the horse to its own devices, he stalked off into the palace, to refresh himself with food and drink, and to spend a blissful afternoon and evening with the maiden.

Otto now felt so triumphantly sure of himself that next morning he demanded to see King Jochem, that he might ask for the hand of the maiden. At first King Jochem refused to see him, sending a message to say that he was indisposed; but later in the morning he changed his mind, and the smirking valet brought Otto into the king's presence.

But what did King Jochem look like! He was propped up in bed, his whole face and both his hands were covered with plasters, and all that was visible of him above the bedclothes was swathed in bandages.

'You see, prince,' he said with an evil snarl, 'I have met with an accident; but I hear that you bore yourself bravely in yesterday's ride over the sandhills, and I also hear that you and the maiden have become much attached to each other. Well, I have no objection to that; but a prince who asks such a priceless gift, must first prove his mettle. Now in the Land of Shifting Shades there lives a monster with seven heads. Go to that land, kill that monster: and on the day that you bring me back his seven heads — on that day you shall wed the maiden.'

'I will set out this very morning,' said Otto.

'So do, so do,' said King Jochem, twisting his plastered face into a wicked grin. 'Take from the stables any horse you fancy. I think not one of them will now try to unseat you.'

So Otto, in high spirits, left the king and went to tell the maiden. 'I feel I could fight and kill a hundred dragons,' said he, 'with such a prize in store for me!'

But the maiden shook her head and looked at him sadly.

'Oh, Otto,' said she, 'there is no such country as the Land of Shifting Shades, there is no such seven-headed monster. King Jochem is sending you on a wild goose chase, and when you are weary with wandering, when you are lost in some desert place, and there lie down to sleep from sheer exhaustion, he will send his devils to cut your throat. We must escape, you and I, we must set out this very evening. Leave me now to make ready for the journey, and as soon as darkness falls I will call you.'

So Otto went back to his own apartments, and the maiden went to the stables, where she had a carriage and horses of her own, and a faithful coachman whom she could trust. Now she told the coachman to wind cloth round the carriage wheels, and to fasten felt under the horses' hoofs so that their going might be silent. And when all was quiet, and a moonless night and a clouded sky gave hope of a safe escape, she went to fetch Prince Otto.

They were just getting into the carriage when the young page who waited on Otto, came running out and fell on his knees before the maiden. 'Oh, take me with you!' he cried. 'Please, *please* take me with you! See, I am so young! Do not, oh do not leave me to grow old and die in this wicked place!'

'Up beside the coachman then,' said the maiden. 'Hurry, and be silent.'

The page was up beside the coachman in an instant, and Otto and the maiden were in the carriage. Now they were driving softly, very softly, out of the palace grounds, and away on the road to freedom, with the padded wheels and the horses' felted shoes making scarcely more sound than the sigh of the wind among the poplars that bordered the road.

All night they drove, the coachman urging on the willing horses, and Otto with the maiden's hand in his, happy as could be. He had faithfully carried out his father's obligation to King Jochem, and now he was going home again, and bringing with him a treasure beyond all price — his beloved maiden.

By daybreak they had reached the frontier between King Jochem's kingdom and King Fritz's. A toll gate and a small guard house, inhabited by an aged soldier, marked the frontier. The aged soldier had just hobbled out and opened the gate, when there came a whirling and a shrieking, and there was King Jochem whizzing through the air towards them. At the sight of King Jochem's hideous scarred face the old soldier fled back into his house, at the sound of his shrieks the horses neighed and plunged. King Jochem made a snatch at the maiden. Now his bony hands had hold of her coat, but the maiden slipped off her coat, Otto thrust his fist into King Jochem's face, the coachman urged the horses through the open gate, and away they galloped, leaving King Jochem screaming with rage, for he had no power outside his own kingdom. He could only stand and scream curses after the retreating carriage. In his wrath he tore the maiden's coat into small pieces, flung those pieces to the wind, rose into the air and, still screaming, flew back to his palace. . . .

So our story comes to an end, with the joyous home-coming of Otto and the maiden, their merry, merry wedding, and their living happily ever after.

9 · What happened to Ivan

Once upon a time there was a lad called Ivan, whose father was a rich merchant. Ivan was good-looking, and Ivan was good-tempered; but — my word! — Ivan was lazy! He didn't like work, no he didn't.

'But you can't spend your life doing *nothing*!' said Ivan's father. 'And here am I all ready to give you a share in my business.'

But Ivan didn't think he was cut out for dealing in merchandise.

'Well then, will you train as a doctor?' said Ivan's father.

No, Ivan didn't think he'd be much good at doctoring. 'You see, Father,' said he with a smile, 'I think sick people might irritate me.'

'Well then — a lawyer?'

No, Ivan was afraid he hadn't enough brains for that profession.

So it went on, Ivan's father suggesting this profession and that profession, and Ivan finding some objection to every one. Until at last his father suggested that he should join the army.

Oh well, if Ivan must do something, he thought the army might suit him. He pictured himself wearing a handsome uniform — a captain or a major, with troops under him, drilling his soldiers and having nothing more to do than to call out *left right, left right. Right about tur-rrn*! (And then, of course, when the drill was over, there'd be plenty of time for fun). Yes, very well, Ivan would join the army.

So his father, greatly relieved, gave him a purse full of money, and packed him off to join the army.

'But don't get any fancy ideas into your head, my lad,' said Ivan's father. 'I'm not buying you a commission. You'll begin at the bottom of the ladder, and if you want to rise from the ranks it'll be up to you to prove your mettle.'

'Oh, all right, Father,' said Ivan. 'I expect I can prove my mettle as well as anybody else. Goodbye, Father.'

Well, as long as that purse full of money lasted, Ivan enjoyed himself in the army. True, he was ordered about, and that didn't suit him; but he made up for it in his leisure moments, treating his fellow soldiers, and finding himself, because of his good looks, his good temper, and his lavish money-spending, very popular. But the money, at the rate Ivan flung it about, didn't last long, and there came a day when Ivan looked ruefully at his empty purse.

What to do now?

'Well, Father has plenty of money,' thinks Ivan. 'I must write for more. But will Father send me more? That's the question. . . . Ah, I have it!'

And he sat down and wrote a letter to his father:

'Dear Father,

You will be glad to know that I am getting on well. Yesterday I was made a lieutenant. But of course now I must have a new uniform, and also I should like to give the fellows under me a little treat. So if you *could* spare me a few coins I should be eternally grateful.

Hoping this finds you well and happy, as it leaves,

Your obedient son,

Ivan'

Oh come now! Ivan's father was delighted. He sent Ivan a bag full of gold pieces; and Ivan celebrated the receiving of it with a feast, at which he got so merry that he began breaking things up, and was punished for riotous behaviour by a spell in prison.

That was all one to Ivan. He rather enjoyed being in prison, because he hadn't to do any work, and he and his jailors made merry together on the remainder of that purse full of gold. But when he came out of prison, and it was *left right, left right* once more, and all the tediousness of drill, not *giving* orders, but having to obey them, and the rest of that purse full of money very soon spent in treating his fellows — ah then Ivan became thoroughly discontented again.

'Can't go on like this!' he said to himself. And he wrote another letter to his father.

'Dear Father,

You will be glad to hear that today I have been promoted again. I am now a captain. I don't know if you will consider this news worth a trifle but. . . .'

And so on and so on.

Back from Ivan's delighted father comes another purse full of gold. And Ivan makes merry whilst the money lasts.

But, bother the money! It seemed to Ivan that it was gone in no time; and it wasn't long before Ivan's father got yet another letter — he would doubtless be pleased to hear that Ivan was now a major.

And Ivan got another purse full of gold.

'The lad's making something of himself after all!' thought Ivan's father. 'All he needed was a bit of discipline — nothing like the army to discipline a lad!'

So now there's Ivan apparently rising from rank to rank, getting at each apparent rise a bag of gold from his father, and chuckling to himself and thinking 'nothing like the army, nothing like the army!'

And then one day Ivan's father gets a final letter:

'Dear Father,

Rejoice with me. I am now a general! But, as you will well understand, a general has many responsibilities, and many expenses; and as I shall not be receiving my salary for some time, I am wondering if you could possibly let me have a little more money to tide me over until pay day. . . .'

'Oh, of course he shall have the money,' thought Ivan's father. 'Of course he shall! But this time I won't send it, I will take it myself.'

And he stuffed a big bag full of gold coins, ordered out his carriage, and set off to pay Ivan a visit.

So now there's Ivan's father, all smiles, enquiring at army headquarters for General Ivan Theobald.

But no one at headquarters has ever heard of such a general.

The only man of that name was a private who was at present in prison again for riotous behaviour and neglect of duty. Would the visitor care to see him? It could probably be arranged.

But the visitor has no wish to see a disorderly private. He wanted to see his son, General Ivan Theobald.

Very sorry, but there is no such person. The gentleman must be under some delusion.

Delusion! How can there be any delusion? Hasn't he his son's letter in his pocket! The indignant father shows the letter. The clerk laughs and laughs. Isn't that just like the rascally private, Ivan Theobald, up to his tricks again!

It took Ivan's father some time to realise how he had been tricked. But when at last he did realise it, he drove off home in a rage, and in a rage wrote a letter to the naughty Ivan:

'You have grossly deceived me. I disown you. From this time forth you may go your own way. I never wish to see you or to hear from you again.'

'Oh lordy, lordy,' thought Ivan when he received that letter. 'What's a fellow to do now? My only source of income dried up! No more feasts, no more fun — just *left right, left right, shoulder ar-rms,* and all the rest of the nonsense! No, I can't stick it. I must run away.'

And run away he did, just as soon as he was let out of prison. Perhaps those in charge were glad enough to get rid of him. At any rate no great search was made, and Ivan was soon over the border and safe from pursuit.

Now of all the money his father had sent him from time to time, Ivan had left but seven gold coins; and the first thing he did, when he came to a town, was to buy himself a ready made suit, which though it was of poor quality and didn't fit him very well, cost five of his precious gold coins. And so, having put on the new suit and tossed his uniform under some bushes, he strolled on his way, came into a big city, and there went into a tavern and ordered a cup of coffee.

But when, in payment for his coffee, he handed the tavern keeper a piece of gold, the tavern keeper said, 'I'm sorry, sir, but I haven't enough small change.'

'Did I ask for any change?' says Ivan, grand as you please.

The tavern keeper bows; the people who sit in the tavern eating and drinking, begin to whisper: 'He doesn't ask for change! He is not what he seems. He must be some rich man in disguise!' And they nudge the tavern keeper and whisper, 'Find out who he is!'

So the tavern keeper goes up to Ivan, bows low, and says, 'Honourable sir, may I ask you a question?'

'Ask away,' says Ivan.

'Honourable sir,' says the tavern keeper, 'I think you are not what you pretend to be? I can see your noble origin in your eyes.'

'Oh ho!' thinks Ivan, 'here's a joke!' And he puts on a grand air and says, 'Well, my man, since you have guessed rightly there is no use in concealment. In fact, I am the King's son. But I am travelling incognito, so that I may get to understand the ways and manners of my father's people.'

'*The King's son, the King's son!*' The people are whispering the exciting news from one to the other. They tiptoe out of the tavern to spread the exciting news through the city; and Ivan, sitting alone in his assumed glory, says to the tavern keeper, 'Fill me a pipe of tobacco. I am now going to the barber's for a shave, and after that to the bath house. Bring me at noon some lunch to the bath house. But,' says he, speaking very haughtily, 'let it be a presentable meal — none of your makeshifts.'

The tavern keeper, bowing again and again, assures Ivan that the meal shall be the best, the *very best* that the town can produce; and Ivan stalks out of the tavern and up the street to the barber's.

The King's son! The news has already reached the barber. He is so thrilled that his hand shakes, and it is a wonder that he doesn't give Ivan a cut with the razor. Ivan, thoroughly enjoying himself, tosses his last gold piece to the barber; and with a 'keep the change', struts out of the barber's shop and on to the bath house, where he takes a seat in front of the fire and spreads out his hands to the blaze.

The bath master has gone to his dinner. In the bath house there is only a servant, sweeping up. The servant is surly; he pushes his broom between Ivan's feet and says, 'What d'you think *you* are doing here?'

'Your question is scarcely courteous, my man,' says Ivan. 'But since you wish to know, I am waiting for the bath master.'

'Well, he ain't here,' says the servant. 'And what's it got to do with you, where he is? I'm here to clean up, and you're in my way — so you best hop it! You go to the devil,' says he, poking at Ivan with his broom.

But just then who should come in but the tavern keeper, followed by two waiters bringing an array of covered dishes; and there is the barber, too, peeping round the door to take another look at the King's son. The tavern keeper and his men spread a table. The tavern keeper, bowing low, and pulling out a chair, asks if his Royal Highness will be now pleased to dine. Ivan takes his seat at the table; and the servant runs off to find the bath master and tell him of the arrival of the King's son in the bath house.

'And I was rude to him, I was rude to him!' cries the servant. 'But how was I to know who he was?'

Here's a pretty state of affairs! What can the bath master do to pacify the King's son? He orders two horses to be saddled, puts on his best clothes, fills his pockets with money, and riding one horse and leading the other, gallops off to the bath house to make the peace.

Ivan has just finished a delicious meal, and is now contentedly smoking his pipe. He is graciously pleased to overlook the insolence of the bath master's servant, and accepts an invitation to become an honoured guest at the bath master's house. But only for a day or two, because, as he explains to the bath master, he wishes to proceed on his travels.

And an honoured guest Ivan remains for a day or so, and then — what happens? The news of the arrival of so important a guest comes to the ears of the Vizier, the chief minister of the country, and the Vizier orders out his carriage and drives off to pay his respects to Ivan.

'My noble lord,' says the Vizier, kneeling to kiss the hem of Ivan's coat, 'I learned too late that you had arrived amongst us, and I learned with pain that you had taken up your abode with the bath master, and not with me. I am surely fallen into disgrace with the King, and with you!'

'Dear Vizier,' answers Ivan with a laugh. 'I pray you not to distress yourself. I had no wish that anyone should recognise me. I had a fancy, you see, to travel incognito, and so learn at first hand the condition of my father's kingdom. But I was recognised in the tavern, and so —' Ivan shrugs his shoulders and laughs, 'my little plan has failed. Now, since I have been recognised, I think it would be my father's wish that I should take up my quarters with you.'

And away drives Ivan with the Vizier in his carriage.

Now in the Vizier's palace Ivan lives in princely fashion. He has an elegant suite of rooms, and is waited on hand and foot. And one sunny morning, as he stands at a window looking out on to a pretty garden, he sees three beautiful young girls playing ball.

'Bless the darlings!' thinks Ivan. And then he has another thought, and he rings a bell, and summons a page, who comes in tiptoeing and bowing.

'I should wish to speak to the Vizier,' says Ivan, 'if he can spare me a moment.'

The page bows again, and tiptoes away. Almost immediately the Vizier arrives at the door and stands there — he, too, is bowing.

'Pray come in,' says Ivan. 'Don't stand on ceremony. You must remember,' says he with a smile, 'that I am still incognito. But those three pretty damsels down yonder in the garden, are they your daughters?'

'Yes, your Royal Highness, they are indeed my daughters,' says the Vizier, beaming with joy because Ivan has called the girls pretty.

'Then,' says Ivan, 'you can give the youngest to me.'

Oh, how the Vizier rejoices! He wants to skip and clap his hands! But he takes a grip on himself, and declares that he is greatly honoured.

'It must be a very quiet wedding,' says Ivan laughing. 'Because, you understand, I am still incognito.'

'Your will is my will,' says the Vizier, ready to burst with joy.

So, without delay, the very quiet wedding was held; the Vizier's youngest daughter, whose name was Elaina, became Ivan's wife; and so good and sweet and charming was she that Ivan, who had married her for the mere whim of the thing, found himself every day loving her more and more.

Indeed Ivan was supremely happy. He asked no more of life but just to go on living with Elaina and loving her. But the Vizier was troubled. He didn't doubt that Ivan was the King's son, because, as everyone knew, the King had a son, whom he had disowned and banished for bad behaviour. So now the Vizier concluded that this son had repented and been forgiven and taken back into favour, and sent out to travel incognito that he might prove his mettle. Yes, it all fitted in nicely. *That* wasn't what was troubling the Vizier! But then — to allow this son to marry Elaina without the King's consent, and whilst the King was away at the wars too! That surely was a misdemeanour that the King might not be inclined to overlook! The King had now come home victorious, and at any moment might hear of the marriage. What was the Vizier to do? Well, clearly the best thing would be to write a letter to the King, confess the whole thing, and pray to be forgiven.

Well, the Vizier wrote his letter, and when he had sent it off, spent an unhappy day or two, waiting for the King's answer. And when the answer came, the Vizier scarcely dared to open the letter.

Ha! He needn't have been troubled! The King, it seemed, was very happy to hear that his son was married, and he begged the Vizier to send his son and his daughter-in-law to visit him.

Now it was Ivan's turn to feel troubled. Heavens, what was he to do? Certainly the King would never forgive him for masquerading as his son. And it had all come about so naturally, and it had been such fun! But the fun, it seemed, must now be paid for: there was no help for it, go he must, and just trust to luck. So he and Elaina said goodbye to the Vizier, and set off in a grand coach for the capital city: Elaina all excited at the prospect of meeting her royal father-in-law; Ivan in the depths of despair, but doing his best to seem cheerful and not distress his darling wife.

That night they put up at a very fine guest house, just outside the capital city, Ivan getting every moment more and more unhappy. 'What on earth am I to do, what *am* I to do?' he asked himself, as he lay restless in bed beside his darling Elaina, who slept so sweetly, so peacefully, with her head resting on his shoulder. . . . 'There's nothing else for it,' he told himself. 'I must run away.'

So came dawn, and he rose quietly from bed. Now or never he must be off!

He bent over the sleeping Elaina. 'Oh, my shining sun, my shining sun,' he whispered. 'No, I cannot leave you. I must rather endure my fate.'

And he kissed her closed eyelids until they opened, and Elaina looked up at him smiling.

'Get up, my dearest one,' he said, 'and dress quickly. We must go to my father's palace.'

So, having breakfasted, off they go in their coach to the palace, to be received most kindly and courteously by the King, who greeted Ivan as his son, and seemed delighted with the charm of his daughter-in-law. But after a few minutes of this genial conversation, the King said he would like a word or two in private with his son, and sent Elaina off to be entertained by his court ladies.

Now, alone with the King, Ivan was beginning to hope that all was going smoothly, when the King suddenly drew his sword and cried out, 'Who *are* you, son of a dog? And how dare you go about pretending to be my son! I have no son, I tell you! I have no son! And for this you shall lose your head!'

'Then I will tell you the truth,' said Ivan. 'There is your sword, here is my head. I know I deserve to lose it. I am a fool. This morning, when I got out of bed, I had quite made up my mind to take to my heels, but at the thought of leaving my darling wife the tears came into my eyes, and I decided rather to die than to grieve her by seeming unfaithful. "If she is to lose me." I thought, "it will not be my doing, but my lord the King's."

The King laid down his sword. 'Tell me your story,' he said.

So Ivan told his story from the beginning, and by and by he had the King laughing. 'For in all my life,' said the King, 'I have never come across a more impudent rascal! Very well, I forgive you. You shall be my son, since never could I have a merrier or more charming one. Now you shall use your wits, of which you have abundance, in my service; and I think my court, which has been but a dismal place, will be the happier for your presence.

'Go, bring your beautiful and loving wife here, that I may bless you both as my children. And as to your own father — heavens help him! — I will see to it that he forgives you.'

10 · The Teapot Spout

'Mother Hannah's Story'

I expect most of you know what a midwife is; but in case there are any of you who don't, I'll tell you. A midwife is a nurse who goes to help ladies when they're bringing their babies into the world. And that's what I am, yes, a midwife.

And I'm going to tell you a story of what happened to me one winter's night. But first I must tell you that I've got a little girl of my own, Norah by name. And for more than a year before that winter's night, my Norah had been limping about with a bad leg, and not a doctor in the neighbourhood could make out what was causing it, let alone cure it.

Well now, speaking of that winter's night. A wild night it was, with the wind high, and great bunches of clouds flying over the face of a full moon — the sort of night one's thankful to have a bed, and not be out wandering. And I'd not long got into bed, and was lying there comfortable with my feet on a hot brick, and my kerchief round my head to keep off the draughts — yes, just dropping off to sleep, I was, when there came a loud knocking on the house door.

'Oh, bother you,' thinks I to myself. 'Oh, bother you! Go away, whoever you are!'

But whoever it was wouldn't go away, they just kept on knocking. So then I got out of bed, opened the window, looked out, and saw down below a man in a dark cloak holding a big black horse.

'What are you wanting?' says I.

'You,' says he, 'and quickly. My lady has need of you.'

Well, then of course I understood, and I bundled on my clothes and went down and out. The next moment we were off, the man astride the horse, me behind him with my two arms round his waist, and holding on tight. And, my word, I had need to hold on tight, for the horse was galloping as I think never a horse in this world galloped before or since. One moment his feet were on the ground, next moment he was up in the air, next moment going through a forest with the tree branches crashing all round us, and the wind roaring in those branches, and the moon appearing and disappearing among them.

So on through the forest and out of the forest, and going through the open gates of a fine palace; and then me off the horse, and up some glittering steps, and in through the great gold door of the palace, and taken by the hand of a maiden in a silver dress, and led this way and that way, and into a handsome room where a lady lay in bed — the grandest bed ever you saw, with pillows of silk and covers of satin, and she crying out with the pains that were on her.

'There, my pretty, there,' says I, 'don't you take on. Nurse Hannah'll see to you' (for that's my name, Hannah).

And I did see to her, and in a short time she'd brought a beautiful little baby boy into the world.

There now, I've forgotton to tell you something. And that is that when I first went into the palace, and was waiting for the maiden in the silver dress to take me to the lady, I was surprised to see, slouching by a pillar, an old neighbour of mine, who I'd never expected to see again, because he'd been lost to sight these many years, and none knew what had become of him. Well, there he was, and looking very glum, and says he to me, 'Hannah,' he says, 'whatever you do, don't you eat nor drink whilst you're in this place, and don't you take any pay for your services, for if you do you'll never win home again. You'll be stuck in this place like myself, who was once brought here to

mend a leak in the palace roof, and got ten gold pieces in payment. Oh the cursed coins,' says he, 'and see here!'

Then he takes ten gold pieces out of his pocket and flings them on the floor: and before you could blink, those ten gold pieces gave a jump and into his pocket again. 'Now I'm their servant,' says he, 'and though they treat me well, it's not like being at home among my own folks. Bah!' says he, and flings the gold pieces on to the floor again. And up they jump, and back into his pocket.

I tell you, it scared me! So, after the baby was born, and they took me into a snug little room and offered me food and drink, I thanked them and said I was on a diet and never ate until noonday. And then I said that if it was all the same to them, I'd like to go home, because I'd my own family to see to, and their lady queen would do well enough now without me.

Then I went back into the bedroom to say goodbye to the

lady queen, who was looking so beautiful and smiling and happy — a real picture she was, leaning up against the silken pillows with her baby boy in her arms.

'Nurse,' says she, 'I am so pleased with you. Go into the next room. You'll find it stocked up with gold and silver and precious stones. Take any coins or any jewels that you fancy, as many as you can carry. You shall have a basket to pack them in.'

Well, I went into the next room, just out of curiosity. And my word — you never saw such a sight: piles of gold coins, piles of silver coins, and baskets full of diamonds and pearls and rubies, and I don't know what all, lying about on every side. I was fair dazzled! But as I went in, so I came out — empty-handed.

'I'm very much obliged to you, my lady queen,' says I, 'but if I were to carry home any of them gold guineas and silver coins and jewels — whatever use would I be in this world? I'd just be sitting dressed up smart with my hands crossed, and drinking tea and eating cakes, and being no earthly good to any of my neighbours when their time came. Why, I'd be dead of boredom in a year!'

'Oh dear,' says my lady queen, 'what a strange person you are! Well, see now, there's wine and cake on the table there, so sit you down and take some refreshment.'

'Oh, my lady queen,' says I, 'it's very kind of you, I'm sure. But I have to think of my figure. I make it a rule never to touch food when I'm out working, because I've a tendency to put on weight, and that won't do in my profession. I have to keep nimble, you see.'

'But I can't allow you to go home unrewarded,' says my lady queen. 'No, I simply can't allow it!'

So then I thinks of my Norah and her bad leg. And I says, 'My lady queen, I have a little daughter at home, and for over a year now she's been suffering from a bad leg, and there's not a doctor can find out what's the cause of it, much less cure her. But I believe you have magic powers, and I believe you've only to say the word to make my Norah sound as a bell again. So if you would speak that word, I'd be more than rewarded for anything I've done here.'

I got a surprise then, because the lady queen frowned — yes, she looked quite angry, and she said, 'Your Norah is a very naughty girl, she has offended me deeply.'

'Offended you! My Norah offended you!' says I. 'Oh, my lady queen, how can that be? Oh, my lady queen, that is quite impossible!'

'No, it isn't impossible,' says she, 'because it happened. And this is the way it happened. You know that on All Hallowe'en we fairies go about the world, and we like to hold our feasts in some houses or other where the kitchen, and especially the hearth, is swept up clean and neat. Well, on the Hallow'en of last year, my ladies and myself were passing by your cottage, and we were delighted with the appearance of the neat thatch, and the whitewashed walls and the clean swept paving outside the door. So we went in. Oh yes, of course the door was locked, but locked doors are no obstacles to us. And when we came into the kitchen we were delighted to find the cheerful turf fire, the carefully swept hearth and floor, the pewter shining on the dresser, and the well scrubbed table. There were some forty-nine of us, but, as you understand, we take up no more room than we wish, so we made ourselves small, settled down comfortably on the floor in front of the fire, spread out our feast, and prepared to enjoy ourselves.

'Well, I had with me my special little ever-full teapot, and I had just set it down after filling all the cups, when your daughter Norah walked in. She was in her nightgown and her feet were bare; and dear me, I admit that her feet are not big as mortal feet go, but one of them was big enough to cover two or three of us. On she came across the floor — what she came for I really don't know or care. But just as I was raising my cup to my lips, down came one of her clumsy feet on to the cup, and spilled the tea all over me. I was very much annoyed, and I seized up the thing next to me, which happened to be the teapot and flung it at her.

Well, there you are, the teapot broke, the spout went into the calf of her leg, and there it is to this day. . . .'

There, that's the tale the fairy queen told me, and you can guess it upset me very much, because you know poor Norah never meant any harm; *she* couldn't see all those fairies sitting about on the floor. It's not a thing you'd expect to find in your kitchen after bedtime, is it? So I shed a tear or two, and went down on my knees, and begged and prayed the queen to have pity on the poor child. I told her I was out working that night (though I can't remember whether I was or wasn't) and that Norah had probably come in to see that the fire was bright against my return, and I said what a good little girl Norah was, and how she always considered my comfort before her own. All this I said to the fairy queen, and now I was sobbing, and begging her to tell me some way to heal the poor child's leg. And when the fairy queen told me to get up from my knees and stop my babbling, I wouldn't get up, and I wouldn't stop babbling, I just went on sobbing, and begging, and imploring.

So at last the queen said, 'Well, well, I daresay you're right. I dare say the clumsy great thing didn't mean any harm, and since you've done so much for me, I won't refuse you.'

Then she gave me a pot of ointment. Where did she get it from? You may well ask — she lying in bed and all! She just snapped her fingers, and there it was in her hand.

'Take this ointment,' says she, 'and rub it on the girl's leg, just where you see a little purple patch. And I hope,' says she, 'you'll remember me with as much kindness as I shall remember you.'

So then I thanked the queen, and put the little pot of ointment in my pocket, and the maiden in the silver dress led me this way and that way, and out of the palace to where the man on the black horse was waiting.

Next moment I was on the horse's back — not knowing how — and the horse was galloping, galloping, now on the ground, now up in the air, and bringing me home just when the sun was rising, and our old cock crowing like a good one.

Norah was still asleep, but I had her awake and sitting up in no time. And I was flinging the blankets off her, and getting hold of her leg, and giving it a good rub on the purple patch with the ointment.

'Oh, oh, you're hurting me!' she shrieked.

But I went on rubbing: and then suddenly I heard a tiny *ping, ping;* and something that looked like a little fiery spark flew out of the child's leg, and went down through a crack in the floor boards. And Norah jumped out of bed, and began dancing about the floor.

'It's gone, it's gone!' she cried. 'The pain's gone! And see, mum, see — my right leg's just as good as my left!'

So then I was laughing, and she was laughing, and we took hands and danced together round the room.

But one thing I told her, and one thing she's always minded since, and that's not to go walking over the kitchen floor after bedtime. Because you never know: if the fairy folk have been once, they may come again — see?